Farmer

BOOKS BY JIM HARRISON

Fiction

WOLF

A GOOD DAY TO DIE

FARMER

LEGENDS OF THE FALL

WARLOCK

SUNDOG

DALVA

Poetry

PLAIN SONG

LOCATIONS

OUTLYER

LETTERS TO YESENIN

RETURNING TO EARTH

SELECTED & NEW POEMS

THE THEORY AND PRACTICE OF RIVERS & OTHER POEMS

FARMER

Jim Harrison

DELTA/SEYMOUR LAWRENCE

A DELTA/SEYMOUR LAWRENCE BOOK
Published by
Dell Publishing
a division of
Bantam Doubleday Dell Publishing Group, Inc.
666 Fifth Avenue
New York, New York 10103

ISBN: 0-385-28228-1

Printed in the United States of America

Published simultaneously in Canada

One previous Delta edition

New Delta edition

March 1989

10 9 8 7 6 5 4 3 2 1

MV

for
Jamie & Norma

Farmer

Imagine a late June evening in 1956 in a seacoast town—say Eureka, California, or Coos Bay, Oregon. Or a warm humid evening in Key Largo or the Sea Islands that are pine-green jewels in the Atlantic south along the coast from Savannah. Imagine that you are in a restaurant and about to order a drink and some seafood. A couple enters. Eyes are raised because to the perceptive the couple are not really ordinary tourists. The woman is attractive, dark complected, ever so vaguely Indian. She is shy and hesitant but cheerful and glances around the restaurant expectantly. She must be in her early forties and has a look of extreme health. To any woman who sews, her clothes would look neatly tailored though simple and made on her own sewing machine. She walks close to the man and hesitates in deference as he chooses a table without the manager's help.

The man walks stiffly with a cane and aims his bad leg as he walks, though this is not important to our identification process. He wears a short-sleeved summer shirt but his tanned arms which are abnormally large and knotted with muscle show the tan only to his elbows and there are three inches of paler skin above them before the sleeves begin. And under the open collar there is a V of pale skin below a neck weathered like old shoe leather. His hair is trimmed short and very close around the ears with a slight cowlick at the back.

The man looks around the restaurant with a wide-faced stare and the indication of a smile. The waitress responds to his order with a shotglass of whiskey and a bottle of beer, a mixed drink for the woman. His speech and gestures gradually become more animated, then he intermittently seems to hope that no one is watching. They laugh and are tentative with a plate of oysters. The man scratches his head, messing his hair. She smiles and reaches across the table, nervously brushing his hair back into place with her palm. He closely examines an oyster shell, rubbing its rough outside surface with curiosity. There is a sense of power in his hands which is magnified by their holding something so slight as an oyster shell. Front to back in the shirt he is thick, chesty with the look of a man approaching middle age who has worked long and hard as a hod

Jim Harrison: Farmer

———

1

carrier or block layer. His face is open and alive. The waitress likes them and returns to their table more than necessary to take advantage of their easy friendliness. The man asks her questions about the ocean that she can't answer. He twists in his seat craning his neck for a look at the water out the dark window. The man eats two desserts and the woman is jovial and talkative, finally comfortable in strange surroundings. They become nervous again deciding what to leave the waitress for a tip. The man peers into a change purse but then opts for a dollar bill and the woman raises her eyes and smiles. After all, they are on vacation.

When they pay their bill the manager thinks the man might be a carpenter but isn't sure. The prescient ones in the restaurant who have eaten much more slowly than the couple have made up their minds. It is a farmer and his wife. And likely from the midwest, as the farmers from the west, ranchers, tend to dress more extravagantly, and those from the east with enough money to travel wear more fashionable clothing.

Out on the boardwalk, though, the couple relaxes and acts oddly like honeymooners. The man gets the tip of his cane caught in the space between the slats of wood. She laughs. They lean against a railing in the breeze smelling the heavy salt low-tide smell. They walk down the steps and across the narrow beach. She holds back as he steps close enough to get the soles of his shoes wet. He pokes at the ocean with his cane, staring at it with the raptness he felt for the northern lights as a child.

Jim Harrison: Farmer

G round ivy, *glecoma hederaceae*, or called gill-over-the-ground: it spread from the pump shed attached to the kitchen out to the barnyard where it disappeared under cow and horse hooves and the frenetic scratching of chickens. There was dew on it now and a yellowish pall from the early June sun barely coming up from behind the orchard. The weed smelled vaguely of dishwater or the slop pail for the pigs. Even earthworms wouldn't live beneath it. Salt or fuel oil would kill the weed, but then nothing else would grow. It was a fact of life.

Joseph looked down at his shoes and the weeds, at his left foot twisted askew. In summer he liked best the first few hours after dawn when the air was still fresh and moist. On hot days he would bathe in the pond at noon, then go down into the cool root cellar and read on a cot beneath a single bare lightbulb. It was a dark and pleasant place with its crates of potatoes, onions, carrots, apples; hung with twine from the ceiling were the last of the bacon sides and hams left over from fall and winter. Sometimes he would read about politics in the newsmagazines, but more often than not he tired of politics and would spend his hours reading about the ocean, general works on marine biology, or popular history books dealing with wars and the Orient. He had never seen an ocean, been to war or to the Orient. He lived on his family's farm and taught at the country school a half mile down the gravel road that passed the

Jim Harrison: Farmer
———
3

house. He figured that some day fairly soon he would see the ocean but the Orient was totally out of the question.

Since last autumn Joseph had been laying the farm to rest, but not with anything as dramatic as a rite or funeral—only a slow and gradual disassembling. The Sunday before his sisters had come to pick over what they wanted from the house; their husbands had wandered aimlessly around the barn, barnyard, toolshed, trying to scavenge something of interest. But they all lived in the city and to them wrenches and garden tools took favor over such valuables as a scythe, harness, corn picker, manure spreader, hay rake. The husbands were aware that Joseph had locked the best of everything in the granary. Arlice, the only absent sister and his twin, lived far away in New York City. To her he had shipped the old trunks with their faded Stockholm decals, bound with straps of tarnished brass, a slight dusty juniper smell inside. The other sisters with eyes for antiques asked "where are the trunks?" to which he replied simply "Arlice."

Frank, Charlotte's husband, had gathered the largest pile of odds and ends and on a trial run had found it clearly impossible to fit all of his booty into the car with his three thuggish children. Frank had been a twenty-year man, a sergeant in the Army, and now kept busy as a plant guard in an auto factory in Flint. He and Charlotte drank great quantities of beer. Marie and Shirley were churchgoers and did not approve of the way Charlotte and her husband drank. Joseph enjoyed watching Frank braying, swearing, kicking everything in sight.

Far off in the corner of the field he could see his neighbor begin to cultivate the corn which was still small and pale in mid-June. Joseph had leased the forty-acre field for a pittance, seeing no point in letting it lie fallow for a year. The neighbor, thinking he sensed weakness, offered a small purchase price which Joseph refused—he would need the land in another year. His neighbor was a pleasant though utterly venal man who worked his wife and sons to exhaustion farming five

Jim Harrison: Farmer
_____

hundred acres. That was what you needed now to make a good living. His own family had stumbled along for half a century on an eighty, only fifty of which was tillable. The other thirty was woodlot and swamp, three small ponds connected by a creek that continued on into a forest that abutted the property. The forest was owned by the state and was made up of some ten sections, over six thousand acres of mixed second- and third-growth conifers, and groves of maple and ash and oak, and ravines and swales, with a large swamp and marsh directly in its center. When Joseph was a child there was still a bear in the swamp but someone had shot it for reasons buried in time. Joseph walked to the woodshed and with his cane nudged an old cowskin rug that hung over the door. In the distance the tractor roared—the simple bastard even cultivated at top speed.

But Joseph was mindful that in another year he would also be on a tractor. Three hundred acres of either soybeans or corn—he hadn't made up his mind. It was only a matter of moving three miles up the road past the schoolhouse to Rosealee's. He pressed his forehead against the cowskin and did not try to resist the image of his student, Catherine, whose body had graced the rug with suppleness and an implacable felinity that would trouble his sleep for years to come. But now he would only have to contend with her in dreams. He had been amused sitting on the stone in the middle of the barnyard on Sunday watching his sisters and their husbands. Though he was forty-three he was their "little brother"; someone who had stayed home, a recluse nearly, who relieved the sisters of their burden of guilt over their mother, whom Joseph had lived with until her death last month. Their husbands considered him a bit strange, a hick; they were affable but guarded with Joseph.

His sisters saddened him. They sat at the picnic table leafing through old photo albums. The dead were always a problem when one leafed through such photographs, something Joseph never did; but his sisters could not resist the al-

Jim Harrison: Farmer

5

bums, though he noticed they tended to skip certain pages by rote. The dead were irresistible, another planet so near but invisible to earth, whose gravity turned and colored the steps of the living. The two children who came before all of them, Carl Jr. and Dorthea dead before the First World War of something mysterious called diphtheria, a word that haunted childhood. Then the father a mere decade ago in 1946 and whom they all with gullibility wanted to believe was "alive" somewhere. Then the mother whose luck ran true only in that she died of causes deemed by all as natural in her seventy-sixth year. Not clipped off earth in surprise as the others, goldenrod before the scythe.

He had drunk too much on Sunday. A nephew he favored had brought Joseph bottles of beer and finally a pint of good whiskey, a present from his oldest sister Shirley, as he sat on his rock in the barnyard. The nephew had lost an eye in an accident and Joseph supposed that gave them some sort of kinship. They hunted and fished together and the boy had once asked Joseph if he could move north from Lansing where he lived with his parents and stay with Joseph and his grandmother. Shirley, Marie, Charlotte had now and then approached the rock where he sat but beyond the usual pleasantries there was nothing to talk about. Joseph and Arlice had been the last of the children and were far enough away, seven years from Charlotte, to represent a different generation. Besides, Joseph and Arlice as twins comprised a secret society that no one entered, not even the most insistent parent or lover.

Late in the afternoon he briefly entered a state where he understood nothing. They had all been young and now they were suddenly old. Thirty years ago they played softball in this yard with their relatives from Chicago, wonderful jolly Swedes who drank too much and brought presents. The corn was high and they ate herring and chicken. Carl was angry— the sow had died for inexplicable reasons—and Joseph and Arlice hid in the well pit where they found a blue racer snake

Jim Harrison: Farmer

———

6

that had fallen in. After Carl's anger had subsided Arlice and Joseph had revived the snake in the horse trough. Then they stood holding the lantern as Carl dug a deep hole and buried the sow. It was such a waste of meat but it might be diseased.

Most farms held few animals that weren't distinctly functional. The game was played too close to the chest to allow for useless mouths. The girls had always had favorites among the pigs so they stayed inside during butchering, though everyone helped during the long evenings of making sausage. Joseph too had been troubled by the problem when young, though he shielded it with a show of arrogance. If a sow had ten piglets in early April within a few weeks you could be sure you would like one the best, usually the runt of the litter. When he was ten his uncle Gustav who worked for the railroad bought Joseph a horse at the auction. The horse was largely a joke in the township; not much larger than a pony, it was obstinate and tried to bite everyone not bringing food. Even Joseph was never sure and was sometimes bucked off for no apparent reason. The horse gave both Arlice and Charlotte nasty bites and his parents wanted to get rid of it but they deferred to Joseph's affection for the animal. The problem was solved for them when the horse got into the alfalfa one night and died of impaction from the rich legume. And there was a succession of not very efficient dogs; their main purpose was to bring the cows in on command and keep stray dogs away from the animals. Joseph's favorite, a smallish mongrel, could climb the ladder to the mow and hide out in the fort with him. The dog loved to nip the butts of the pigs when they protruded from the slats of the pen. It made the sow angry and she would charge squealing at the dog who knew he was protected by the fence.

As he drained the last of the whiskey it had occurred to Joseph that even the rock he sat on gave him cause for reverie: it had seemed so large when they were children and used it to climb onto the pony; now it had shriveled, was sinking into the ground, and Joseph leaned hard on his cane, flushed with vertigo. Then Rosealee drove into the yard to say hello to his sisters and he squinted his eyes against the late afternoon sun. She was disappointed that he had forbidden her to tell the sisters of the planned marriage but he didn't want the emotional mess that would have come from the announcement. Joseph wanted Rosealee in the car and halfway from northern Michigan to the ocean before they would stop in some anonymous place and be married by a justice of peace. Then she could call who she liked on the phone.

Against the blurred periphery of the setting sun he had watched them talk and they became ageless—it could have been June in 1936 instead of 1956; Shirley, Marie, Charlotte, Rosealee—only Arlice was missing but he invented a shadow for her in the dim light next to the lilacs. When Rosealee approached, Joseph had found himself in a rare public act of affection: he lifted her hand and kissed it. She was taken aback, then gazed at him with longing. How could he have so nearly destroyed their love like some madman burning a barn or shooting his animals? He felt that if he had not been sitting on the rock he would have disappeared from the agony of the year. But he knew that the nature of his life wouldn't permit so simple a departure barring suicide—that the pivotal year that had begun so easily with the grace of last October would not slip unhaltingly into the past as had so many of the years before.

Jim Harrison: Farmer

Joseph liked the long cool sunny autumn days when even the shadows on earth were clean and specific. The barn created a larger darker barn and the tines of the rusty hay rake were magnified across the surface of the weeds. The first hard frost had flattened the rank foliage in the garden revealing the plump acorn and summer squash, the leftover cucumbers and tomatoes rotting. The geese and chickens owned their running scratching shadows, and Catherine's horse had a brother gelding flat and rippling to the ground as it moved for shoots of grass. Standing with one foot inside the shadow of the boulder near the fence Joseph waved his long arms toward the geese who spooked at the shadow. The oldest approached and honked fretfully at him as if to bawl him out. She was long past the eating stage and spent her days chiding the other birds and chasing any barn cats that entered her field of vision.

The shame of it was that Catherine was his student. It had started on a warm October day when she had brought her horse over to store for the winter. He had agreed to board the horse after she told him that her father would make her get rid of it unless she could board it cheap. She was a senior and extremely sassy and bright. She enlivened many dreary days, for which he was grateful. Her father was a retired Army major who had just moved his wife and daughter north the summer before. Joseph liked him immediately. So well in fact that he had introduced him to some good fishing spots. Trout fishing

Jim Harrison: Farmer

9

was the major's passion, to the exclusion of his gibbering alcoholic wife. The major felt a tenderness toward his daughter, though, and Joseph felt uncomfortable at the idea that Catherine might tell him about Joseph.

The flirtation had really begun with the first day of school. But then Joseph had always flirted, then refused to do anything about it for the obvious reason that a serious flirtation could only end in marriage in these parts. There wasn't much fooling around. People paired off, whether young or old, and finally married. Everyone knew that someday Joseph and Rosealee would marry though it appeared Joseph was spending a half dozen years making up his mind. Never in his twenty years of teaching, though, had he made love to a student.

So Catherine had said she would bring the horse over Saturday and Joseph had insisted she do so by noon as he had planned to go grouse hunting after doing the chores that always piled up for Saturday mornings. He had sworn all morning because it was unseasonably warm which made the hard walking of grouse hunting even more difficult. He liked it best in the forties and fifties, not in a hot swamp when even the mosquitoes came out again for Indian summer.

Catherine showed up after lunch full of apologies. He showed her the stall he had prepared for her horse, which was a fine chestnut gelding. Oddly he had seen her only in an over-the-knee-skirt and she looked very sexual in her tight riding jeans. He showed her around the barn and was uncomfortable looking at the flex of her butt as she climbed into the mow. At the top of the ladder she turned around, looked down, and noticed his discomfort. She was so much more vivacious and sophisticated than any of his students had ever been. She was from the outside world and this clearly interested him no matter how dangerous the situation was. Deep inside he excused himself in advance. After all it was his last year.

They walked out the back door of the barn discussing payments for hay and oats. Her face was mildly flushed and she

Jim Harrison: Farmer

———

10

loosened and retied her hair into its ponytail. She slipped off her boots and stuck her toes in the pond. Joseph dumbly sat down beside her.

"God it's warm for October," she said. "You know I just loved that Keats poem you read yesterday." She knew Keats was Joseph's favorite. On Friday afternoons they heard poetry whether they wanted to or not. The entire five upper grades. Through the partition you could hear all the younger ones shrieking and Rosealee's cries for order. Sometimes Joseph would go in and cow them with a look. Now he verged on saying "a season of mists and mellow fruitfulness" but he caught himself and said jesus christ instead.

"What?" She looked at him. He looked down at the water and her feet.

"I think we should make love," he said. His voice was matter-of-fact though his head felt hollow.

They re-entered the barn and spread the old cattle blanket on the loose hay behind the stanchions. She quickly shed her clothes and they were just as quickly finished. Joseph lay back and wanted a cigarette but he never smoked in the barn. She began chatting about Keats again, then about her horse who had been watching them with no particular curiosity. Maybe he had seen this all before Joseph thought. She stood and cooed at her horse offering him a handful of oats. Joseph stood behind her with his hands on her buttocks. She turned and smiled at him, then knelt down.

It was mid-afternoon before he dropped Catherine off on his way grouse hunting. The major was out in the yard and they chatted diffidently about hunting and the weather and Catherine's horse. Catherine said good-bye and sauntered into the house as if tired from a long ride.

"She's a smart girl," Joseph said.

"I'm proud of her. She's been moved around so much but she's turning out fine." The major lit his pipe. "Would you like a drink?"

Jim Harrison: Farmer

11

"I would but I want to hunt until dark." They shook hands and Joseph dragged his leg to the car.

The hunt took place in a trance that occasionally lapsed into panic. Once while taking a rest he walked off and left his gun propped against a stump. He was embarrassed as he retrieved it even though alone. He walked very slowly and missed several birds because he was distracted. After each missed shot he would yell shit. He came to his favorite place, a hillock in a grove of oaks overlooking a creek, and threw himself down meaning to nap. He shielded his eyes from the sun but his hand smelled of the light touch of the perfume she wore. He was thirsty and walked down to the creek to drink. Three grouse flushed in the clearing across the creek but he had left his gun on the hill. He watched their graceful curving flight into the swamp and yelled shit again, this time with all of the power of his lungs.

Back up on the hill he sat for an hour and thought how unfair it was. Though in his early forties he had made love to only a few women and with the exception of Rosealee they had been disappointing. One of them, a whore in Grand Rapids, had even laughed at his leg. The others had been furtive contacts with the mothers of students and a single drunken encounter with the wife of a friend. With Rosealee it was sweet and pleasant, precisely what he imagined it would be like to be married to someone you deeply cared for.

But Catherine when she sat beside him on the drive to her house turned him into a lunatic making him think of the hundreds of novels he had read, written he always believed by liars because he had never until Catherine experienced anything remotely similar except in his imagination. It more closely resembled a fit than anything else. He laughed at the thought and smelled his hands but the scent of the grass and ferns where he lay had covered her odor. He thought with sadness that he had made love to this girl more in an afternoon than he usually made love to Rosealee in a week. Perhaps to

Jim Harrison: Farmer

——————

12

release him from any natural guilt Catherine had assured him as she dressed that she had taken lovers before. She really enjoyed herself she said. He felt merely stupid on the cattle blanket which scratched his bare sweating back. How can she be so naked and nonchalant, her breasts rising chafed and pink from the rough blanket, turning, bending to pick up her underpants. He reached for her again but she had to get home she said because her mother wasn't feeling well and she had to drive to town for groceries. Sitting on the hill he felt young and stupid. And then sad that he had not until this afternoon found out that on very rare occasions life will offer up something as full and wonderful as anything the imagination can muster.

Jim Harrison: Farmer

J oseph had always spent a great deal of time trying to think analytically about his main preoccupations, which were fishing and hunting. As the years passed he found he had less and less interest in the mere act of acquiring fish and game. For instance he no longer shot ducks. Not only were they easy but they were simply too fascinating to watch on the beaver pond way back in the center of the state tract. If you spent a long time on your stalk you could get close enough to watch them for hours. It was much more difficult with Canada geese, surely the wariest of all birds. But the ducks, most commonly mallards, mergansers, teal, or blue bills, would complacently swim and speak their odd language. Joseph experimented in alarming them. Sometimes it required only an upraised hand wagging from cover but if they were feeding avidly enough you could stand and shout before they would flush. The geese always kept several scouts on the periphery of their feeding area to alert them to any danger.

On the Sunday morning after his meeting with Catherine he sat by the pond for a couple of hours watching the birds, and the peacefulness of sitting so long amid this beauty drew him to questions that seem essential to everyone. An idea that fixed him to one spot was that life was a death dance and that he had quickly passed through the spring and summer of his life and was halfway through the fall. He had to do a better job on the fall because everyone on earth knew what the winter

Jim Harrison: Farmer

was like. The ocean creatures he read of illustrated the point so bleakly. To devour and be devoured. But their sure instincts kept them alive as long as possible, as did those of the wild ducks before him, or the geese. Even the brook trout, the simplest of the trout family, were mindful of the waterbirds, the kingfisher and heron, that fed on them.

One afternoon he had been lucky enough to see a Cooper's hawk swoop down through the trees and kill a blue-winged teal. The other ducks escaped in a wild flock circling the pond twice while the Cooper's hawk stood shrouding its prey with its wings. Joseph watched it feed on the teal's breast then fly off to a large dead oak to preen. It was far too spectacular to be disturbing. *Once in town he had seen a car turn a corner and strike a lady pedestrian. He could still see the shocked, twisted look on her face.* A couple of hours later a few ducks circled the pond hesitantly. Soon they had all returned to their feeding.

For Joseph there were presentiments of the troubles to come even before he had begun his affair with Catherine. He had left half the apples unpicked and for the first time didn't want any school children in the orchard. What little heart he had left for teaching was gone before the end of September; he met each morning feeling a certain dread mixed with lassitude. He spent far less time in the tavern playing cards and far more time reading about distant places. All of the strictures, habits, the rules of order for both work and pleasure seemed to be rending at even the strong points.

October grouse season had always been the high point of his sporting year along with late May and early June and the heavy mayfly hatches of trout fishing. He would rush home from school leaving Rosealee to lock up, change his clothes, and hunt with old Dr. Evans until the fall light disappeared. He would hunt all day Saturday after the chores were done and on Sunday from dawn to dark. But this year the doctor had decided to give up hunting—his legs would no longer take the strenuous walking. The doctor had presented Joseph with his fine Parker shotgun in August: Joseph had coveted the expensive gun for years, the beautifully grained whorl of its walnut stock and the fine engraving of a pointing dog along the breech. But when the season began this time everything conspired against him: the weather was cold and wet, making his leg ache more than ordinary, then the weather changed into an over-warm and humid Indian summer, and grouse were near the bottom of their seven-year population cycle, though woodcock were plentiful.

It was a male woodcock that pinpointed a certain loss of nerve. After sunup one Sunday he walked along the west fence border of the farm, back toward the corner where the creek and swamp joined the state property. It was a splendid morning with white frost on the pasture; clear, cold, with the ferns finally dead and the walking easy. He approached a blackberry swale and for a moment pretended he was gesturing his old bird dog, a springer spaniel, into the blackberries to flush the birds. But the dog was long dead. Joseph stood there and stared at a weak sun climbing over the swamp. A woodcock flushed at his feet toward the sun and he lost it for a moment but then it dipped below the treetop and he dropped the bird easily. He walked over and picked up the bird but it fluttered in the tall canary grass, still alive. He caught it and began to wring its neck but the woodcock's large brown eyes followed his movements. He turned the bird around but the bird twisted its neck toward Joseph still staring at him with a glint of the morning sun shining off its retinas. Joseph closed his own eyes and snapped its spine near the neck. He shoved the bird into the game bag in his vest but he was trembling.

Joseph sat down on a pile of old fence posts and thought about the woodcock. How could he become so nervous after thirty years of hunting? He had never looked into a bird's eyes before and it had at least temporarily unnerved him. He tried to

Jim Harrison: Farmer

———

16

ignore how nearly human the eyes looked, but he couldn't rid his mind totally of the idea: eyes are what we hold most in common in terms of similarity to other beasts. He always cringed when he hooked a fish in the eye. When they slaughtered both cattle and pigs the eyes stayed open in death. But it was more than that; the woodcock was warm, palpable, it quivered, and its eyes did not blink under his gaze.

By mid-morning he had bagged two grouse but had missed several woodcock. He sat on a stump near the creek and slowly ate his sandwich, wondering if he had missed the woodcock on purpose. They were normally far easier to shoot than grouse. Did it mean, too, that one more pleasure was to be denied him on his already severely atrophied list of enthusiasms? He had sensed that the energies that fed his interests had somehow diminished but he believed these energies would recover and persist. Only it wasn't happening and the near frenzy that had occurred with Catherine the week before was the first "new" thing to enter his life in a long time. Sitting there on the stump with the sun warming his back and drying the dew from his pant cuffs he felt bovine, immovable; he numbered his passions: he had loved Rosealee for thirty years, he had hunted and fished for thirty-five years and worked hard on the farm nearly that long, almost assuming manhood at eight when he learned to walk again, and he had taught twenty-three years though that was more menial habit than passion. You had to count reading about subjects that were least in touch with his own life. But these simple things had truly filled his life and he knew them so intimately that an edge of panic entered him on considering that they might simply blow away like clouds. He could not comprehend it; the earth looked the same and this October day was not unlike a hundred other October days. He looked at the odd way his heels wore off his boots because of his walk. Even the stump was a familiar chair. Should he blame the woodcock's eyes or Catherine's body or his own fatuous brain for losing control? He looked at the fence which

Jim Harrison: Farmer

17

was in disrepair and again felt guilty about the apples. How many blankets had his mother quilted for his marriage to Rosealee? Why did he drink more and read less, and why did his favorite books bore him? He knew in some oblique way that he was no longer his father's son. He despaired that forty-three was too late for new conclusions, but he knew this was a lie. One of the doctor's favorite speeches when he was drunk was how grief made people lazy, torpid. Joseph wanted to believe that that was only the doctor's profession, that the doctor was vaguely buggy from seeing so much death. But it was too easy to remember the necessary deaths of so many of the farm animals he had been close to, how even the execution of an awful, cantankerous rooster had touched him.

On the way back to the house he shot another grouse. The grouse flushed toward him and flew low over some sumac. He made a difficult shot and that warmed him somewhat. Now there was enough for dinner. Rosealee was coming for dinner and he looked forward to their comforting though pointless conversations on whether he should begin farming full-time next year. They had accumulated a stack of equipment catalogs but the catalogs were far less interesting to Joseph than books on the ocean. He was startled by an urge to throw the woodcock into the weeds in order not to have to look at it again. But he hadn't fallen apart that much. To waste game was the ultimate crime: he despised hunters who shot crows for what they called "sport" or under the assumption that crows fed on duck eggs. Crows stayed on the farm the year round and after decades of studying their habits Joseph believed the crow to be the sole bird with any wit.

The unnerving incident followed him around throughout the season and the more he tried to erase the image of the woodcock the more insistent its presence became. He looked into the eyes of a dead grouse and felt nothing. The doctor thought of grouse as small gray chickens that flushed wildly and flew at fifty miles an hour. But they were without much

Jim Harrison: Farmer

18

character; if a chicken fed on wintergreen, chokecherries, wild grape, it would taste as good as a grouse. Grouse were splendid dinners wandering around in the forest waiting to be gathered and eaten. Now Joseph removed woodcock from this food category and allowed them to join the highest strata, that of the owls and hawks, the raptors, harriers, and *Falconiformes*. This made hunting much more difficult and his average bag dropped to the level he owned as a neophyte; he could no longer "point shoot" on instinct at the flush but had to wait an extra split second to make sure it was the gray flush of a grouse rather than the golden brown of the woodcock. His mother no longer asked him, how many, Yoey? when he came in from the hunting, noticing the irritation in his voice when he replied.

Jim Harrison: Farmer
———

One evening at the tavern the game warden confided in Joseph that he had seen a coyote in the country. Coyotes were assumed to have totally disappeared, moving north where they were safe from the irate farmers who blamed them for all sorts of impossible predations. The game warden had followed the coyote with his hound and pinpointed what he thought was the general location of the den for Joseph.

He was excited about the presence of the coyote, and that night he set about devising certain stratagems on just how he might approach the animal. Perhaps he would build a blind but that was rather obvious. He remembered that he and Orin had once called a fox upwind of their hiding place by using a predator call, a wooden whistle that purportedly imitated the noise of a dying rabbit. He got out of bed and searched among his hunting things, an assortment of old shotgun shells, licenses, an inoperable pistol, a kit for carving your own gun stock. It wasn't there. It had to be in Orin's trunk. He walked out to the kitchen and dialed Rosealee.

"Rosealee this is me. Can you look in Orin's hunting trunk and see if there's a wooden whistle? Not a duck call but it looks like one. It makes a shriek."

"Joseph! It's two o'clock in the morning." She sounded vexed.

"Please just check." He did not care what time it was. He

drummed his fingers and lit a cigarette. There was a hideous squeal on the phone and he nearly dropped the receiver.

"Is that it?" she giggled.

"Bring it to school, OK? I love you."

"I love you, Joseph."

The next morning Rosealee gave him the whistle with a quizzical look. He fondled it in his sportcoat pocket and at midafternoon during a biology test absentmindedly blew on the whistle and startled the students.

"How many of you know what this is?" He was embarrassed and tried a cover-up. "None of you? Well it's a predator call." He blew on it again, this time on purpose. "When an animal is in distress it gives off a call out of pain and desperation. Dogs whine and snarl. A hooked fish emits signals and in the ocean this attracts sharks and barracuda. Out west if a fawn bleats it might draw a mountain lion. Human beings scream. This whistle imitates a dying rabbit and with it I hope to see some fox and hawks at close range."

He continued lamely for a while then told them to go back to their tests. Daniel, his most obtuse student, waved his arm frantically but Joseph would entertain no questions. Something in the corner of his memory nagged him. "Human beings scream." Not really. Those photos in an old life that he could never dispel from his memory; they were not unlike his schoolchildren playing softball, but in the photos the children playing ball were lined up outside the gas chambers at Belsen. Dietrich who worked for the dairy in town said at the tavern that his people were filthy animals but Joseph said to my knowledge animals do not behave that badly. The Germans weren't going to eat the children and Dietrich was drunk and wept. Nobody wants to know those things so why make pictures out of them?

After school Joseph drove directly to the log road that would bring him closest to the area the game warden thought most likely for the coyote's den. He was still troubled by chil-

Jim Harrison: Farmer

———

21

dren, though he readily admitted to himself they could be a source of anger and sometimes needed paddling. But a half-dozen times over the years children had come to school severely beaten and twice he had taken them to Dr. Evans who exploded with rage. But there was no one to protect children from parents with mental problems. Nothing in Joseph's mind approached the horror of a brutally beaten child. The worst case involved a broken arm and two cracked ribs on a hyperactive little girl of seven years. She claimed she fell down but Joseph knew her father, a mean-tempered sheep farmer. When Joseph saw him at the tavern he drew him aside and said your daughter won't admit you beat her because she loves you but if she comes to school all bruised again and says she fell down I will figure out a way to kill you. It will be easy. You'll be found in a field with your goddamn head blown off.

Joseph took his gun from the trunk and walked off through the forest without changing his clothes. He laughed at what an odd sight he would present if anyone were around; a gimp schoolteacher in a sportcoat and his Sunday shoes and necktie shuffling through the woods with his shotgun. He heard the hammering sound of the pileated woodpecker, a bird the size of a crow but timid and wary of humans. Joseph read that the Indians had killed them for their feathers at one time. Maybe that's why they kept themselves from human sight; fear of their enemy had entered their genes and was transmitted over hundreds of years down to the present. He scrambled panting up a hill and along a ridge. Now over the tops of the trees he could see the small field in a valley a quarter mile away. On the other side of the valley was a rock outcropping covered partially by wild grape vines. Below the outcropping the grass was tall due to a seep, a small spring that kept the ground wet. Joseph became stealthy and moved slowly toward the edge of the field. When he was a hundred yards away from the outcropping but still inside the woods he blew the whistle lightly three times. It was eerie, as if some warlock were bleating, but sharp enough to carry to any predator within a mile.

Jim Harrison: Farmer

Joseph sat there until dusk, mindful that the coyote might have seen him and simply be wondering why a man would sit in the brush three hours blowing on a whistle. He stretched his mind for a fresh stratagem. He could tie a chicken to a stake out in the middle of the field. They had only three hens left but he could swipe one from Rosealee. It was dark and cold by the time he reached the car. On the way out he had managed to tear his trousers on a windfall and to get his shoes wet and muddy. A grouse had flushed and he had shot at the noise for no reason, fire belching from the barrel. He shouldn't have done it he thought driving home: perhaps the coyote would move his den. He would try the predator call for a week, each day from a different vantage and if it didn't work he could always resort to staking a chicken.

"Yoey you're a mess. What happened to you?" Her eyes were wide with surprise. "Clean up and have some supper. Are you drunk?"

Joseph laughed at his bedraggled appearance in the mirror. His wet shoes squeaked and he could see his knee in the hole in his trousers.

"Rosealee called. She said you were out looking for a coyote. There aren't any coyotes around here any more." She came to the bathroom door. "You're becoming a little crazy. You should get married."

She had roasted a mallard that one of his students had given to him. It was stuffed with rice and fruit and nuts and she had glazed it with plum jam. For a moment he was disturbed by how little she had eaten and how much she had been aging lately. There was a large vase of zinnias on the table that she had picked before the frost could ruin them. As he ate the duck Joseph stared at the zinnias as if he were seeing flowers for the first time. The light behind them cast a shadow and he thought that it was certainly the first time he had noticed flower shadows.

Joseph spent a fruitless week on the coyote, reaching a

Jim Harrison: Farmer

point of despair where he thought he might shoot the damn thing if he did see it. One afternoon he cleared a sandy area and left a piece of chuck steak, but the next day there were only crow and raccoon tracks. He found the den at the far end of the outcropping but he couldn't be absolutely sure it wasn't a fox den. Finally on Saturday he staked one of Rosealee's chickens at the far end of the field about thirty yards from the woods and spent hours glassing the chicken with his cheap binoculars. Arlice had sent a fine pair of binoculars but he hesitated to use them for fear of damaging them. He saw no contradiction in this stupidity.

The chicken flopped and squawked for an hour then nestled down quietly in the grass, probably, he thought, out of shock. Two red-tailed hawks circled high above as if intent upon a meal. Joseph rushed from his hiding place so the hawks would see him and leave. He had barely gotten back to the woods when he turned and saw a brown blur. The chicken was gone. Jesus. Why hadn't he used a solid stake instead of a stick? When he reached the place there was nothing but the small stake hole poked in the earth. He began laughing at the idea that he had been watched all the time. He searched the area near where he had been sitting. Fifty yards up the hill he found several scats that resembled dog shit. The coyote had obviously been watching him during the week. Joseph could almost see through the coyote's eyes as he laughed with the embarrassment of an amateur: the man sits there restless and stares for four afternoons. He leaves some meat which is not eaten because I'm not hungry. He leaves a lovely white chicken. He runs and waves at hawks and I circle around the clearing. As he walks back to his hiding place I run out and steal the chicken.

Joseph resumed his grouse hunting with vigor though he still consciously avoided shooting woodcock. Rosealee and his mother were pleased with his apparent return to normalcy. So

Jim Harrison: Farmer

was the doctor who had rather expected an occasional grouse for dinner. One evening the doctor stopped by and Joseph's mother set another plate for dinner. She had stewed a hen and made biscuits. Joseph did not know it but the year after his father died, the doctor and his mother had even discussed marriage one summer evening on the porch. Joseph presented the doctor with three uncleaned grouse he had shot that afternoon. The doctor liked to hang his birds a few days after the fashion of the English and French.

"About goddamn time. I thought you were being cheap but then I called your mother and she said Rosealee said you were hunting a coyote. Why do you want to shoot a coyote?" The doctor had finished his second plate of the chicken and biscuits and worriedly contemplated a third.

"I wasn't going to shoot it. The game warden said there was a coyote back near the lake that he tracked with his hound and he kept it secret so no asshole would shoot at it. I wanted to see a coyote. Never saw one before." Joseph felt lame about his reason for not grouse hunting.

"Did you see it?" The doctor took his third helping and drank deeply from a glass of beer. The meal was worth the incipient indigestion.

"For about a tenth of a second. It took a chicken I baited it with. But it was like not seeing it at all."

The doctor told how he was once fishing in the Wind River area of Wyoming and he looked up and far above on the side of the canyon two dogs sat on a rock peeking at him from the brush that surrounded the rock. Only they weren't dogs, they were coyotes. They were curious about what he might be doing standing in a river waving a stick.

Jim Harrison: Farmer

25

Joseph admired the frayed, energetic look owned by an active farm. Often the lawn wouldn't be trimmed and the house and buildings not recently painted but there was a peculiar grace in the battered implements, the huge manure piles, and great fertile fields. He despised the farms near town that had been bought up by the managerial class of the sheet metal company in the county seat. After the war the company had grown swiftly by manufacturing aluminum products for windows and house trailers. Those who possessed the best jobs bought the farms within a few miles of the county seat and let them lie fallow or turned them into pasture for their children's horses. Some of the land was sold to build look-alike homes for the workers. But the farm houses would be modernized and false shutters added. Sometimes white board fences would be built and the outbuildings painted a bright red. Maybe they were trying to make it resemble Kentucky or New England.

When the county board held a hearing on the closing of his school Joseph had been asked questions by several of the new people. One asked how he could teach without a college education, to which he replied that he wasn't teaching the farm kids any college courses. The audience had laughed and the questioning became more pointed. Joseph had been angry and announced that he wouldn't answer any more questions because they had already decided to close down his school anyway. And he didn't care because he was tired of teaching. He was sorry for the students who would have a forty-mile round trip on the bus. They had to do chores in the morning and evening and would find it hard to compete with the kids in town. Then as an afterthought (he had had a few drinks) he added that they all struck him as pompous assholes and he was leaving the meeting in order to catch the second movie.

This was shortly before Thanksgiving and during the brief vacation the county school superintendent had called him frequently to get the apology the board demanded. Joseph refused. Then the day after Thanksgiving the superintendent had stopped by in his deer hunting clothes. Joseph let him in the house only because the man had known his father.

"Just out this way hunting and thought I'd stop by." He refused a drink.

"No you weren't," Joseph said. "Your boots are dry and I heard you got a buck the second day of the season." Joseph poured himself a drink. "You're out here trying to get me to apologize to those pompous assholes." He laughed. "How much did your deer dress at?"

"Just short of a hundred thirty, a little old for good eating." He was pained, wanting somehow to trick Joseph into an apology, however mild.

"There's no way," Joseph said, reading his thoughts. "I only got six more months and I'm not going to kiss ass."

"It wouldn't be kissing ass to avoid trouble. You were out of linc."

"I don't care. How could I say I'm sorry if I'm not? Even if I did they'd know I wasn't sorry so what's the point? You run the schools, don't you?"

"What will you do if they say I have to fire you?" The superintendent had become profoundly uncomfortable.

"I'm not sure. I got an old fishing friend who's a lawyer. I guess I'd sue on the basis that there's no rule that says I can't call an asshole an asshole. Tell them that. They never gave me

Jim Harrison: Farmer

27

a good reason for closing the school. We could always have another meeting and I could call them shitheads this time." Joseph laughed loudly. "Why did you bother to put on those clothes?" He laughed again.

"This is not really a laughing matter, Joe. I'm disappointed in you after all these years." The superintendent stood flushed with impatience.

"Oh go fuck yourself. I taught hard for over twenty years. What kids of mine that went to college did well, few as there were. Just get out of here. I don't have time for you or people like you." He looked out the window at the softly falling snow. He couldn't remember when he had felt so utterly bored with life.

"I'll give them your message, Joe. I'm sorry." The superintendent opened the door.

"What are you sorry for? That you work for assholes?" Joseph was laughing again. "I feel sorry for you but don't bother me again with this horseshit. I got six months more and I want them to be peaceful."

When the superintendent left Joseph's mother peeked around the door. "You shouldn't talk like that to an educated person," she said.

The issue was never formally dropped but Joseph received no more pressure from the superintendent. For the first time since Joseph began teaching no one from the county office visited the school during the Christmas pageant. Rosealee was a little disappointed because her sixth graders had painted an immense mural of the Holy Land though it had been more or less copied from a *National Geographic*. She wanted someone "educated" to see the mural. The local parents who bothered to stop by only joked about the blue horses and white camels and said the Christ child looked like an "aaa-rab" or, funnier yet they thought, a "nigger." But Rosealee had more patience than Joseph with the stupidities of the parents which were passed on so comfortably year after year, from generation to gen-

Jim Harrison: Farmer

eration. Rosealee accepted them as they were and made great efforts to register some change, however small. Joseph's tactic was merely to stare with unconcealed contempt. But they all knew Joseph was somehow one of them, no matter how strange and removed his behavior. They knew his parents and sisters, the dimensions of the family farm, who his relations were, how the family fared during the Depression and the war. Most of all they knew that Joseph was only accidentally a schoolteacher, that were it not for his withered leg he would be an average, unsuccessful farmer like his father: someone who tended to fish and hunt when he should have worked his land a bit harder. The older, more conservative farmers liked to make jokes about Swedish farm practices, though with the passing of years some of the best farms in the county were owned by Swedes who themselves made jokes about their poorer relatives.

During Christmas vacation Rosealee was very happy to receive an offer to teach in town for the coming year with a rather hefty raise in salary. And Joseph got a letter that pointedly stated that his teaching services were no longer needed by the county. He was thanked in falsely hearty tones for his twenty-three years of dedicated teaching and if he wished he could come in to the office and fill out application forms for substitute work, though of course education rather than seniority would be the basis for hiring. Joseph was amused at the stilted texture of the language. He was also pleased that he would be able to withdraw the monies that had been taken out of his pay over the years for retirement. That would be enough to make a trip to the ocean.

That evening Rosealee and Joseph drove to town to have dinner at a restaurant, an event that took place no more than twice a year. Joseph was pleased to get out of the house because his sisters were visiting with their families. He spent much of his time in the barn or in his workshop in the granary, but it was cold and his nephews and nieces drove him batty. He looked at them as awful city children and potential

Jim Harrison: Farmer

pyromaniacs intent on burning down the barn and abusing Catherine's horse. Only his favored nephew met his approval and they rabbit hunted for days on end until the freezer was overloaded. Joseph and his mother liked fried rabbit but his sisters thought it trashy.

Rosealee acted restrained on the trip into town as if any obvious cheerfulness over the job offer might upset Joseph. But he was happy and mostly talked about the ocean. He had pretty much decided to see the coasts of Oregon, Washington, and California. Florida would be too hot in the summer. Maybe he would visit Florida in the winter if the money held out. He would fish and study the marine life all day every day. Only a tent, a Coleman stove, and a box of books were needed. He wanted to see a manta ray, thinking it the creature on earth least resembling any other creature.

At the restaurant Joseph immediately noticed his main enemy on the school board, a woman about his age. She pointed out Joseph to her husband. The husband frowned. Joseph grinned at them maniacally and waved. Rosealee was embarrassed and studied the menu. The food was usually awful though described in glowing, ornate terms. Joseph didn't look at the menu because he always ordered shrimp and a saltwater fish even though he knew both had been frozen for months. But they were from the sea, and had a salt smell to them, however vague. He always drank rum in this restaurant though he didn't care for the flavor. Rum was somehow exotic, coming from the Caribbean, a place he thought of in travel poster terms: white beach, deep blue water, fish, lovely women in scanty bathing suits. Hedy Lamarr or Dorothy Lamour lolling in the water drinking from a coconut.

"Our mothers think you should farm." Rosealee announced this from the blue, calling as she always did her mother-in-law "mother."

"What farm?" Joseph returned abruptly from the Caribbean and looked at his soggy grayish shrimp covered with its blood-red sauce.

Jim Harrison: Farmer

"Both farms. You could hire someone to help."

"Oh bullshit. It'd take fifty grand in equipment to even get started which is fifty grand more than I got assuming I want to try it anyhow. I almost would have to tie my goddamn foot to the tractor clutch. Tell them to mind their own business. They always use you to get at me." Joseph scraped the sauce from the shrimp. It killed the smell of the sea he thought. The woman was staring at him again and he made a crazy face in irritation.

"Well mother is heartbroken that nobody works it." Rosealee was insistent.

"Let her lease it. There's more profit in leasing it. I'm not going to be some gimp farmer to please them."

"I guess they think you'll fall to pieces without your job. You know, drink and not marry me."

"Who's talking about marriage? You can find somebody better when you take your new job in town." He slipped his hand under the table and squeezed her thigh but she was morose and only toyed with her food.

"Maybe I should find somebody else. But I got six years into you." She attempted a smile.

"Likewise. We should make up our minds."

"I already have. Six years ago. You're a bit slow."

He smiled. They had talked like this for years beginning shortly after Orin's death. Things had been improving the past few weeks but Joseph supposed it was because Catherine had gone to Atlanta for the holidays with her parents. He was getting some rest. It embarrassed Joseph that he used his thoughts about Catherine to excite him before his perfunctory lovemaking with Rosealee. He had never had the opportunity to explore his thinking on human sexuality very deeply. Arlice had mischievously sent him a book by Henry Miller and a book by D. H. Lawrence as a present. He had read blatantly dirty books before but they didn't impress him. Miller and Lawrence however wrote beautifully about sex and Joseph felt melancholy about his age after he read these censored books.

Jim Harrison: Farmer

31

He had missed so much in life. He felt he should have dragged his weary leg around the earth instead of staying on the farm grieving over his dead father and his mother whose health had begun to fail.

"What will change if we marry? I don't want to live with Orin's mother and you don't want to move from that fine house into ours."

"Of course I do. I'd move in tomorrow. Robert could live upstairs or maybe even stay with mother."

Rosealee knew that the slightest mention of Robert, her son by Orin, irritated Joseph though he saw Robert daily in school. It was incomprehensible to Joseph that Robert so closely resembled his father physically, yet so utterly lacked Orin's boldness and humor. Robert lived in some sort of post-pubescent trance, always vaguely pained, yawning, sulking, whining.

"I said Robert would stay with mother."

Joseph wasn't attentive. He was studying the bones of a fish advertised as "pompano." The bones were disappointingly similar to trout bones. Someday he would see the bones of a whale and the teeth of a shark. That would be better than cultivating corn twelve hours a day in the hot sun. Or taking care of cattle which were milk and shit machines and drove him crazy with their obtuseness. Pigs were smarter. What would a shark do to a swimming pig? At the movies he had sat through a short subject about sharks twice, returning the next evening to sit through a boring movie to see the sharks again.

One day Rosealee asked him if he still liked her at all. During the late fall and early winter, they had been spending at least two evenings a week together, if only correcting papers, listening to the radio, or simply talking. But as his mother's illness advanced he had had less taste for any company except Catherine's, so he was startled at Rosealee's question thinking she might know something. They made love quickly and Rosealee left the house looking not all that much happier. She wasn't fooled.

On the verge of sleep, it seemed strange to Joseph that he had known Rosealee for thirty years. *I was thirteen and Dad and I were mushrooming after fishing. We saw a small shack near the state land and stopped to talk to a man who looked dark as a Mexican. He lived so close to the swamp there were mosquitoes in broad daylight but he didn't seem to mind much. We sat on a log talking. It was a freshly peeled white pine log with amber-colored beads of resin coming out the cracks. He was cutting pulp for the paper mill and had the pulp lease for some state land. He called Rosealee Rosealee make us some lemonade and soon enough out came a girl with three glasses of lemonade. The girl was brown and pretty and about thirteen years old. She wouldn't say hello and Dad and the man laughed when she ran back in the house. I was embarrassed for no reason and stopped hearing them talk. We gave the man*

Jim Harrison: Farmer

some fish. He didn't want morel mushrooms because he had already picked a lot with Rosealee who had threaded them and hung them up to dry. Thanks for the brook trout. Dad gave him six large ones and he said no, four is enough my old lady ran off years ago there is just us.

So that fall Rosealee came to school and became friends with Arlice and was around a lot. I let her ride my horse. And Mother gave her clothes the other girls outgrew and sometimes she made dresses for her because she didn't have much of anything and Mother pretended they were old dresses. Rosealee would cart over a whole bunch of jams and jellies she made from wild raspberries, blackberries, huckleberries, chokecherries. She was young but knew how to cook. She read our books and magazines because they only got Michigan Farmer *which no one but Dad read. If you have to do it all the time you don't want to read about it. The girls all bitched because they had to hay but I worked too with only one good leg and the bad one hurt a lot then. Now it doesn't hurt. Some kids at school said Rosealee was part Mexican because she could get a tan from the sun even in winter but Rosealee said to Arlice that she thought her mother might be part Indian or her father said part Cree. He met her up in Minnesota though she was from Montana but she didn't like Michigan and took off with another man when Rosealee was three and couldn't remember. But Rosealee had a strange necklace in a little box that Arlice said was magic. I had a box full of arrowheads I picked up behind the plow but Rosealee just blushed when she saw them because she was tired of being teased by everyone. I beat up two guys in eighth grade for calling her squawface mostly because Arlice coaxed me to. Then Dad had to come to school to talk to the teacher with me and the other parents because the guy's neck was wrenched. Afterward on the way home Dad said you have to forget name calling because everyone does it and he used to be called dumb Swede and all Swedes were called dumb Swede by some people.*

When they were fourteen Arlice and Rosealee thought they were grown up and started wearing bathing suits when they swam except once when we rode way back in the state land and swam in a beaver pond. When I dove down the water was so clear but I didn't find where the muskrats entered their house. The girls watched and I promised not to look if they wanted to swim so they giggled and came on in. Rosealee's butt was quite white so her coloring was mostly tan. That was the first time other than child's play which is silly, the first time I was really interested in girls and their sex. But they were the ones making the big deal out of it that day. Then suddenly we all talked about it and Arlice and Rosealee said they weren't going to go all the way until they were sixteen. I wanted to hide my head and think about it but then out of nowhere I said that I had done it at the fair when we all slept in the cattle barns, but I had only almost done it. They took me a lot more seriously then and when they kept asking questions I only said you'll find out soon enough. Then the only time I touched Rosealee until Orin died so many years after, in fact a week after Orin died, was one night when Mother and Dad had a pinochle and polka party and we snuck some whiskey. Arlice was necking with her boyfriend and I necked with Rosealee but she kept her pants on to be safe. Then she started going out with Orin and that was that right up until the war when he was a pilot in Europe. They married just before the war then Orin was gone for four years. I was best man at the wedding. Orin came home and farmed some and then he was called to the Korean War and crashed into the China Sea.

Maybe Catherine is what she is to me because I've known Rosealee too long and there are no surprises. Or she chose Orin first because I had a bad leg and had to be a schoolteacher. I don't think so. Orin was a great person. A better bird shot than me though I was best at fishing. Orin was always poaching deer which Dad didn't like though he was happy when Orin dropped off a bloody package of fresh veni-

Jim Harrison: Farmer

———

son. Fried with onions. Dad doesn't know that Orin is dead because he died first a few days after V-J Day. I doubt the dead know each other. Does Keats know Fanny in death? I know Catherine is a secret conniver and ultimately no good but who said a woman, a girl, has to be good for you to like her and want her? Also she flat out screws like a lunatic. Maybe I'll make love to Rosealee those ways and see what she does. Maybe she and Orin did it all those ways and she won't want to because it will make her sad. I'll try anyway.

I want to see a shark. I always wanted to see Keats's grave but I'd rather see a shark and the ocean. I'm tired of looking at photos of the ocean. Or The Blue Lagoon *with Jean Simmons on that deserted island out in the Pacific, swimming around in clear blue water just living on fish and coconuts. Rosealee's thing is as tight as Catherine's forever who cares. Their breasts are the same though Rosealee's belly is nicer and so is her skin. Sometimes Catherine moves so much I don't last long. Rosealee likes to eat grouse and venison and Catherine thinks it's stupid and brutal to go hunting so I told her to shut her mouth when she doesn't know what she's talking about. Mother will die.*

The thought of his mother's death brought Joseph wide awake. It was the first year of his life that he had had trouble sleeping and both his mother and Catherine were the causes. *My god the mind is strange. And too much whiskey with little sleep doesn't help. Maybe there are ghosts after all though they surely have human forms.*

Jim Harrison: Farmer

36

In mid-December they had three days of wind, bitter cold, and drifts mounting up against the north sides of the house and barn. Then in the middle of the night it was suddenly so silent he awoke. Half of a moon made the field outside the window bright and clear. A large dog stood in the middle of the field. It looked toward Joseph's darkened window then slowly began walking toward the house. It disappeared in the hedge, then he heard scratching at the door of the pump shed. Then a long circular howl. He hurried downstairs and turned on the yard light. But it was the dog he had owned as a child thirty years before, given him to console him after the accident. Then one night the dog had disappeared, probably shot as a stray. But now it stood on the edge of light on a drift and they stared at each other. Then it vanished. Joseph ran out into the snow in his bare feet calling the dog's name. He tripped and fell on his face in the deep snow. Perhaps he was sleepwalking. He returned to the house and started a fire in the kitchen stove. He filled a pitcher with cold water, took out a bottle of whiskey, and listened to country music until dawn. As the bottle's volume dropped he had intermittent fits of weeping.

Jim Harrison: Farmer

J oseph spent New Year's Day in the granary trying to revive some old harness that had been neglected for the ten years since his father's death. The harness was stiff and moldy and the silver fittings tarnished black. He was in a violently bad mood from the night before. He and Rosealee had gone to the annual New Year's party at the tavern and had stayed until closing which on New Year's Eve was four a.m. rather than two like the rest of the year. Rosealee continued the quarrel over farming: Orin's mother had offered her savings to get them started. She was very old and had no use for the money which Rosealee would get when the old lady died anyway. But Joseph had been boozily adamant and when she continued to push he had yelled at her and the tavern had fallen silent, the polka band stopping in alarm. Joseph had hobbled out to the porch during the pause and had stood there in the sub-zero air breathing deeply. The doctor had followed him out and talked idly with him about fishing. Then Rosealee appeared weeping and shivering without a coat and the doctor had bawdily suggested that she must truly be in heat to put up with such a bastard. That changed the mood and they walked back into the party. Joseph insisted that Rosealee dance with everyone which she rarely did because of his bad leg. Joseph and the doctor were so intent on planning a fishing trip to Canada for the coming summer that they scarcely noticed the arrival of the new year.

Jim Harrison: Farmer

———

Joseph fed the pot-bellied stove split wood, and stood occasionally to watch the blustering wind blow snow across the barnyard. It was bitterly cold and the snow was dry, forcing itself in flour-soft drifts against the barn. Too cold and windy to rabbit hunt or ice fish. And the neat's-foot wasn't bringing back the harness which had cracked from neglect. He would have to soak it in a large quantity of oil but it would never be serviceable again for anything but decoration. He remembered Tom and Butch, the last team they owned before his father's death. They were a pretty well-matched pair of Shire-Belgian crosses, bay colored and weighing about a ton apiece. They had won the pulling contest at the fair two years in a row and before the accident plans had been made to campaign them at other fairs. Joseph's eyes blurred with grief when he thought of the teams his father had owned. There had been a glorious brood mare named Belle when Joseph was eight and was convalescing from his injury. Belle would let him lie along her back while she wandered around the pasture or went down to the creek to drink. Joseph would chew on an oat sprig and forget about his pain, held aloft by her great broad back and sweet horsey smell. His mother feared further injury but his father sensed that it was the sole thing that made Joseph happy. He would ride around for hours like that, even through summer rains that made Belle's back slick. Then he would hold gently to her mane. Once he rode through suppertime and his father had walked out to get him in the far corner of the pasture. His father carried him back in the dusk and he wept because he saw his father was weeping.

Joseph was startled by a knock on the granary door. Catherine pushed in followed by blowing snow. She had on a new fur-trimmed parka.

"Here I am!" She put her arms around him then quickly took off her coat. "How's my horse?"

"About as good as a horse can be in winter." Joseph was glad to return from the past though he had decided that he and Catherine had to stop fooling around.

Jim Harrison: Farmer

"How was your Christmas? Look what I brought you."
She drew a small crockery jug from the large pocket of her
coat. "It's twenty years old. I had Daddy get it."

Joseph held the jug reading the label. "Sour mash bourbon," he said aloud.

"Taste it." She sat on the arm of the chair and kissed his
ear.

"Not now. I'm too hungover. You want to see the horse?"

"Not now. I'm too sexed up," she said mockingly. "Look
at my lovely new underthings." She had unbuttoned her
blouse revealing a pale blue bra.

"Wait a minute." Joseph's resolve was disappearing. He
uncorked the jug and poured some whiskey into a coffee cup.

"Look at these. I knew you'd like blue," She had slid
down her jeans so he could see the blue panties. She giggled
and turned so he could see the backside.

Joseph drank deeply and sighed. There was really no point
in making her unhappy today. He lifted the cattle skin blanket
off the wall of the grain bin and spread it near the stove to protect them from the cement floor. He found that his hands were
trembling. He turned off the lamp and the room was dim in the
pale wintry light though there was a flicker of red through the
grate of the stove door. He knew his mother would leave the
house. She'd been feeling ill and had an appointment for tomorrow. He suddenly felt old and very melancholy taking off
his clothes while watching the snow furl in clouds across the
yard. Catherine's tracks were nearly covered and the windshield of her father's Jeep was white.

He stuffed some more wood into the stove noticing that the
shadows had lengthened and the kitchen light in the house was
on. His mother would be fixing supper. Catherine was dozing,
curled up to the stove as close as possible without burning herself on its iron legs. Their odors mingled with the wood smell
and the musty cattle blanket. He poured himself a small drink.

Jim Harrison: Farmer

He meant to slow his drinking. It had lately gotten out of hand for the first time since his father's death.

"Time to get up." He nudged Catherine with his toe. She yawned deeply and stretched. He impulsively turned on the light, to see her better after two weeks of privation. He felt now that he needed at least a month to break it off. He wanted to indulge himself. It was so much like the novels and he wanted to totally enter the reality of it before he came to his senses.

"I heard you got fired," she said as she dressed.

"Not exactly. This is the last year for the school." He was bored by the subject and she noticed his diffidence.

"Let's get married in June and just take off." She put on her coat and hugged him. "I hope the Jeep isn't stuck."

Jim Harrison: Farmer

Joseph had begun to lose interest in deer hunting soon after his father died and well before he had ceased killing ducks. Again, the prey was too easy for him after so many years spent walking and riding on horseback through the several thousand acres of state land. He had come to know precisely the habits of the deer in every season. Deer were much more predictable than most hunters thought. If you figured out where and how they moved it was only a matter of getting downwind of their path. Despite their caution they came irrevocably into the rifle sights. So deer hunting had become a form of not very involved trickery as Joseph's skill grew with age.

Animals in general had fascinated him all his life. When young he had fed the pigs ham and was rather startled when they ate it with the same vigor as the potato peelings, corn, or other garbage. He felt embarrassed about tricking the pigs. And the quiet way that a playful calf became in months a heavy somnolent feeding machine soon to be milked or slaughtered for beef. The mare easily mated with the stallion, her son of three years back. Animals were so clearly just themselves, much more so than humans. He liked the idea that man was the only mammal that thought of himself as part of a species. The porpoises he dreamed of seeing seemed most like humans in this sense of self-awareness. There was even some evidence that some porpoises committed suicide.

Joseph could trace to the minute when he had decided to

stop hunting deer. A single day in February had clinched his attitude. For several nights he thought he had heard hounds baying from the forest followed by the harsh barking of other dogs. Then a storm came dropping a half foot of new snow and interrupting an unseasonal thaw with new drifts. On the following Saturday morning Joseph walked through the swamp to the place he knew the deer yarded for protection in the winter. He found seven carcasses spread through the swamp, some chewed over and three with only their throats torn open. A small clearing was scarred with dog and deer prints and frozen blood. He felt angry with the dogs, most of whom had become feral with neglect. Often they were joined by neighbor dogs that returned in an instant to more ancient instincts for the kill. The hound must have been the redbone that had come up missing the previous fall. A coon hunter had stopped by the farm several times to make inquiries. Joseph liked the man, a factory worker from Lansing, because he rarely shot a raccoon but called off his hounds after the animal had been treed.

Joseph felt sluggish looking at the carcasses. They were scattered around the clearing and he hoped he wouldn't find more. In former times he would have acted more quickly, even to the point of riding out at night and firing into the air. He felt weak and stooped near a doe to catch his breath. He touched one of her eyes and found it frozen solid. He rubbed his hands along her frozen stomach which no doubt held a fawn. He was not so much disgusted with the dogs as he was with the people who didn't take care of them.

When he got back to the house he called the game warden and discussed what to do, though a plan had already been forming in his mind. The game warden offered his help but Joseph insisted that he could take care of it. That night he set the alarm for two hours before dawn and told his mother that he would probably be back soon after daylight. There had always been a number of feral dogs around but he had never seen one in daylight, only their tracks in snow or sand. Years before they had lost three sheep and had sat up the night after waiting

Jim Harrison: Farmer

for the dogs to return, but against his advice Carl had insisted on taking a thermos of coffee which on a cold night could be smelled by any mammal a mile away. And the doctor had been frightened while fishing the Pine River to see a row of large rather gaunt-looking dogs watching him from a clay bank in a particularly wild area. When they followed him downstream he had been alarmed enough to call the game warden in Manistee who said nothing could be done about the dogs in the large forests. When the dogs were contained in a smaller swamp the local hunters would try to drive them out once a winter and shoot them. Joseph suspected that many of the predations blamed on coyotes were in fact caused by feral dogs. He had never met a farmer who could tell the difference between coyote and dog tracks.

When the alarm went off and he dressed in the dark he was happy to see that the moon was shining bright and clear. He picked up his rifle and cattle blanket in the pump shed but was a little disturbed when he stepped into the barnyard to see how still the night was—not even the faintest breeze to cover any noise he might make. He had lost to the stillness the advantage he would have had by approaching that neck of the swamp downwind. He tied an old gun strap to the blanket and set off across the frozen ice and fresh snow as if he were going to sow oats by hand.

It took an hour to reach the place he had in mind but it proved to be too far back in the poplars from the clearing to afford clear shooting. He crawled closer and unpacked and spread the blanket behind a log that would make a steady rest for the rifle. The neck of the swamp protruded into the clearing where two of the carcasses lay. He hoped they would be hungry enough to feed off the frozen carcasses but doubted it. Fresh game was easy this time of year when the severity of February weather made the deer the easiest mark conceivable. The deer population had been unusually high with all the food available in the new growth that had sprung up after several cuttings of timber for lumber and pulp. Their numbers in-

Jim Harrison: Farmer

———

creased vastly if there was a succession of two or three light winters.

Lying there waiting Joseph felt a sharp pang of loneliness for Carl who had been dead ten years. It was strange how one could go along for weeks, months even, feeling nothing and then something would set the grief off again in a wave. Now it was the cattle blanket beneath him. They had always spread their lunch on it when ice fishing and if it was cold and windy enough they would make a small lean-to out of a tarpaulin. So he would be happy to be here tonight, only I would have to keep him from drinking his coffee or even Guckenheimer, the smell of which is far stronger.

The first baying of the hound shocked him and he looked around wildly trying to get relocated after his reverie. He shivered and strained his eyes toward the far edge of the clearing and the dark wall of trees. There wasn't enough light to see his watch but he had followed the path of the moon as it passed through the spare contorted branches of beech and figured it must be close to dawn. Then the hound bayed again, sounding closer this time, and a bluejay screeched, disturbed from sleep. Another dog barked, then yelped, and he heard a thrashing in the brush. There must be at least two of them, he thought, blowing on his cold hands and noticing he could see them better than before. There was a pale tinge in the east and the first hint of a breeze a little warmer against his face than the night air had been. He heard more thrashing in the brush across the clearing as if an animal were wheeling and circling in the same place. Now as the prey was cornered the hound's baying turned to a steady yelping and there was deeper snarling from another dog.

Joseph wiped the moisture from the scope of his rifle and sighted at the noise. He saw the tip of a tag alder sway and then the deer suddenly broke into the clearing, breathing deep and hoarsely with fumes of steamlike vapor coming from her mouth and nose in the cold morning air. He put the deer in the crosshairs of his scope. She was dragging a hind leg and began

Jim Harrison: Farmer

bleating like a sheep, as badly wounded deer sometimes do. He repressed an urge to shoot her and relieve her misery. Then the first of the dogs entered the clearing and he was surprised to see it was a spaniel he recognized from several miles away near the lake. He sighted on the spaniel's yipping head as the dog approached the deer as if pointing a bird, but then the hound sprang into the clearing with an even larger dog that resembled a German shepherd. The deer faced them with no resolution. The scope was misting from his breath and he wiped it. He flicked the safety and shot the shepherd in the neck and hit the startled hound in the chest as it stared at the source of the first shot. The spaniel raced across the clearing and Joseph swung on it but changed his mind. He lacked the heart to shoot a bird dog. He swung back on the shepherd lying still in the snow, then on the hound who was quivering. He shot the hound again and it lay still. Joseph was startled to see the deer standing there with head raised, breathing heavily as if nothing had happened. Then she swung her head and stumbled back into the woods. He was sweating and exhausted as he walked back to the house.

Joseph tried to imagine a time when Michigan wasn't a game farm for hunters, when the natural predators, the puma, wolf, coyote, and lynx still lived there. And the Indian. Not man hunting for sport and his house pets gone wild and utterly destructive. But this wave passed and he was swept back into memory seeing the farm in the distance in the dawn light with a trail of drifting smoke coming from the chimney over the kitchen wood stove. What pleasure it had been when company came in winter. He and his sisters would talk excitedly *company is coming* and they would get up early to make the house sparkle. It was usually on Sunday and they would go to church in the morning then come home and wait in their best clothes for the relatives and their children to arrive. Sometimes it was the doctor and his pale wife, who died soon after Joseph's accident without having borne any children.

Jim Harrison: Farmer

Rosealee's mood did not improve. One evening late in March Joseph promised to take her to the movies at the county seat. It was Friday and ordinarily they did something together to celebrate the end of the school week. Joseph drove over the frozen mud ruts of her driveway with a sort of energyless foreboding. He had spent the hour after school and before dinner in the car with Catherine. She had said that she had to talk to him and couldn't wait, which left him giddy throughout the afternoon over the idea she might be pregnant. When he read poems aloud last hour he stumbled over his favorites; "swollen streams" became a seventeen-year-old girl's pale swollen stomach. Oh my God, he thought, with the guilty urge to head for a far place, some island in the ocean. Zanzibar would be ideal, at least the *National Geographic* rendition.

But his premonitions had proven false. Catherine had only announced that she intended to go to drama school and hadn't decided on New York or Chicago. Joseph could have strangled her because they had never met in daylight without the horse ruse. After she asked for his opinion and got only his silence and a sigh of relief she reached for his trousers. He stopped her hand, wanting to drive a little farther on the forest road if it wasn't too muddy from the thaw or if there were no drifts left to form barriers.

"You scared me." He gunned the car through a puddle of

Jim Harrison: Farmer

slush. She raised her eyebrows. "I thought you might be pregnant."

"I wear a diaphragm, silly." She pulled his ear, then began giggling. Soon she was laughing hysterically and this distracted him enough to get the car stuck in a rut. He told her to shut up, and rocked the car gently out of the mud.

"How about that first time. Did you have it on then? I mean in October?" He backed the car into what looked like a safe, dry place. He often parked here grouse hunting and for a few moments he wished he were grouse hunting and had never met Catherine.

"Why should I tell you?" She began laughing again. She knelt on the seat, raised her skirt, and deftly took off her panties, slipping them backward over her shoes. He always wondered how she could manage this act so gracefully. Perhaps there had been many rehearsals.

"I just wanted to know. I don't want to play the fool." He brushed her hand away. "I'm not doing anything until you tell me." He lit a cigarette.

"OK you grouchy bastard. Yes I was wearing it then. My mother had me fitted for one in Atlanta when I was sixteen. When I first saw you in class I knew you loved the arts as much as I did and I was lonely and I liked the way you looked. So that Saturday I saddled the horse, then remembered you had at least looked at me in a funny way a few times, so I went back in the house and put it in in case you might want to make love to me. Satisfied?"

Suddenly Joseph began laughing and his bad mood evaporated out a crack in the steaming windows. "You must be the only girl in the county that's got one. Where is it?" He was curious about what they looked like.

"Inside me, dummy!" She pressed his hand against her.

Now in Rosealee's driveway with a fine sleet ticking off the window he dreaded the evening. His ailing mother had roasted a chicken and he had eaten the whole thing, stuffing

Jim Harrison: Farmer

and all, plus a monstrous drink. He frankly needed a nap and feared the night's activities closing in. Friday was their special evening on the parlor couch while her son Robert wandered around in town. Her aged mother-in-law slept in the bedroom above the parlor but she was nearly deaf. Once they had made love during the boxing matchs, the Friday night fights on the flickering television. Chico Vejar versus Chuck Davey. Rosealee never permitted lights on and the blue light from the TV was sexual. He found himself slipping on the porch then stumbling in the door.

"You're going to break your neck. Is it icy? What were you doing out in the car?"

"Thinking. Yes, it's slippery." His last idle thought had been why Catherine wanted to do it so often. She could talk about poetry one moment and the next she'd be hissing and groaning.

"Maybe we shouldn't drive to the movies. What do you think?"

Joseph looked around the big living room. It always hopelessly reminded him of Orin. The house was large and solid, much better than the house he lived in. Orin's father had been bitter about his wife's bearing only one child. Joseph's dad would console him with the fact that he got only daughters and God had injured his son's leg. Sometimes Orin and Joseph would sit on the tavern porch on Saturday afternoons and try to overhear their fathers. They both knew that Orin's dad had a girl friend and thought it very mysterious.

Rosealee waved her hands in front of his eyes, startling him. "What's wrong with you?"

"Maybe I got the flu." He sat down heavily.

"You've had the flu for months. You're acting strange and I don't think it's your mother." Her arms were folded and her voice bleak.

"It's a change of life." Joseph spoke calmly. "Men my age go through a change of life. They know they're going to die without doing what they wanted. I read an article about it."

Jim Harrison: Farmer

49

"Oh, bullshit!" She was angry. "What do you want to do other than screw a movie star like everybody else?"

Joseph laughed. Rosealee never swore unless she was extremely upset. Now her eyes flashed. But more sadly, he thought, she sensed he was slipping away from her after so long.

"What do I want to do? I want to spend some time on the ocean. In a boat and swimming. Where it's warm and there are no people, no students, only fish and water. I don't want to teach any more but that decision's been made. So I want to spend a few years around the ocean just reading and drinking and fishing."

"You really are a dumb Swede." Her voice was softer, sensing that he was acting very odd and serious. She went into the kitchen and got him his glass of bourbon and water without ice.

"I also want to fuck you in the broad daylight." His voice tightened and his eyes looked at her unsteadily. He had never used the word in her presence. "I'm tired of fucking you in the dark Friday and Sunday nights and sometimes on Wednesday. I want to fuck you with all the lights on or in broad daylight doing everything I ever thought of."

"Is this what happens when a dumb Swede reads too many novels or drinks too much too long?" She tried to lighten the mood but he grabbed her arms.

"Look at me. We're forty-three and we've never fucked in the daylight let alone seen the ocean. We've been to Washington once but never New York. We've never fucked outside except we almost did thirty years ago. I think we should act different before we get old and die and it's too late. Don't you want to act differently? I'm tired of you acting like a goddamn widow. It's been six years. I'm tired of fucking a widow in the dark. I've loved you since I was thirteen." Joseph drank his whiskey in three gulps and tried to stand but felt weak.

"I'm so sorry." Rosealee wept. "I'm so sorry I disappoint you."

Jim Harrison: Farmer

Joseph abruptly got up and she stumbled against the chair to get out of the way. He turned on the ceiling light and three lamps. He drew the drapes and began taking off his clothes.

"Other than my leg which you've seen a hundred times while swimming, do I look so goddamn strange I have to be stuck in the dark all the time like a goddamn snake? Look at me now."

Rosealee looked around the room fearfully, as if God were watching the scene, or her mother-in-law or dead husband.

"You're not looking and you haven't answered." His voice rose then cracked on "answered." He felt dizzy and for a moment wished he hadn't taken off his clothes. But it was too late to do anything but plunge on. "I want you to fuck me like you did Orin at sixteen or twenty or twenty-five. Like he told me you did. Like you and Arlice talked about, laughing all the time. I don't want to just fuck a sad widowed schoolteacher then die in the winter."

"Oh, shut up, please shut up." Rosealee's eyes flashed then she started crying again. "You're crazy." She paused, feeling somehow girlish, as if she were doing something naughty in the barn or woods with Orin and they had narrowly escaped being discovered. "Let me think a minute." She rushed into the kitchen, her head pounding. Now she did feel strangely girlish and excited. She drank from the bottle and coughed.

Joseph looked down at his stomach, member, and twisted leg. He looked odd to himself in the bright light. He heard Rosealee put down the bottle and cough. "Bring me a drink," he yelled. "If I have to stand here all evening I may as well have a drink." Drinking is cheap magic he thought, noticing a scratch Catherine had left on his thigh. He had asked her to trim her nails but supposed she wanted to leave a mark.

"All the way?" Rosealee came into the room in her bra and panties and handed him his drink. She stared at the floor and blushed deeply.

"Absolutely everything." Joseph felt giddy as if he were

Jim Harrison: Farmer

51

remonstrating a pupil. "And hurry up with it." Now that he had the upper hand totally he meant to keep it. He drank slowly and watched her unhitch her bra and toss it on the couch. Their eyes met and they both were somber. Joseph thought that she looked much more interesting than he had expected, more definite somehow than Catherine's easy nakedness, almost muscular from working hard since a young girl.

"Well here goes." She stepped out of her panties then looked vacantly at the ceiling.

"Now we can get started," he announced. He walked in a slow circle around her, poking here and there as one judges cattle. He was disarmed by the way her body shook with laughter.

"This is fun," she said.

Joseph awoke on the floor covered only partly by an afghan. The hall clock said four a.m. The ceiling light buzzed. He stretched from his cramped position and looked at Rosealee stretched out on the couch on her belly, still nude. She was snoring lightly and her back had collected some lint from the rug. Joseph stood by the couch and stared down at her bare bottom, cementing mentally what had happened hours before. He leaned down and kissed her neck, then on a sudden impulse covered her once more. She kept her eyes closed but managed to lift his weight until she reached her hands and knees.

When he finally reached home it was dawn. He had driven the three miles with the car lights out and had been startled to see four deer standing in the road. Then he turned the lights on and the deer stood for a minute transfixed as they always did. He never understood why they did this as it got them killed so often by both moving cars and the poachers, the jacklighters who aimed their rifles down the flashlight's beam. What a sleazy way to kill an animal. He regularly called the game warden when the poachers were in the area. It had once caused him some trouble when a violator got on his back in the tavern,

Jim Harrison: Farmer

52

accusing him of being responsible for his getting caught. It was a former student, now in his thirties. Joseph was playing pool with the doctor and on being pushed too far had cracked the lout hard across the knees with the cue, sending him to the floor.

Now he stood in the barnyard outside the pump shed door. The neighbor's rooster crowed and the milk truck rattled down the section road. The wind from the north that had brought the sleet the night before had switched around to the southwest and had warmed. The air had the smell of another false spring. True spring never reliably came until early May and until then it was best not to expect much from the weather. Joseph thought idly of how many years he had gotten up at dawn to do chores, or well before dawn to do the milking so he could go trout fishing. Only after summer parties had he occasionally stayed up through the night. He had never felt so exhausted and it wasn't the easeful exhaustion of having worked long and hard in the field. He noticed that his mother's bedroom light was on so he went in.

"Joseph?" Her voice was thin. "I made some coffee. Please come in. Did you feed the birds?"

"Shit, I forgot." He poured a cup of coffee. They kept a few chickens, ducks, and geese. Other than Catherine's horse they were the only animals left on the farm. The last cow had gone dry the fall before and he had given it to a poor family to slaughter. His father had been stupid about animals, always looking for a combination out of which some profit could be wrung. While most farmers stuck to a single breed of cow, Joseph's father had moved improvidently from Jerseys to Holsteins to Guernseys, thus never building up a profitable dairy herd. He was simply too whimsical, preferring Poland China pigs to the better Chester Whites because he liked the name. It was obvious to the other Swedes in the farm community that his people had been fishermen in Sweden before they emigrated, not farmers.

"Joseph?"

He numbly escaped his reverie and walked to her bedroom

Jim Harrison: Farmer

in the gathering light. There was a thin line of red out the east window.

"How are you feeling, Mama?" He leaned and kissed her. Her Swedish Bible was open on the bed beside her. He didn't know the language and wasn't curious.

"Very badly. It feels like there are nails driven in my stomach." It wasn't a complaint but a statement of fact. "You have to marry Rosealee if you are going to sleep all night with her, Joseph. You weren't brought up to act this way."

"I know it." He felt shy before her biblical authority.

"Rosealee told me the other day that she didn't think you wanted to marry her. I told her nonsense. You were just waiting for me to die so you wouldn't have so much on your mind."

"Maybe I'll marry her in June. People get married in June a lot." He wanted to get off the hook, feed the birds and go to bed.

"That's so they can have a spring baby," his mother laughed. "You're not thinking of babies at your age? But I had you at thirty-nine. Carl wanted to try again for a son. He was so happy when you came he bought a frilly nightgown for me." She laughed again.

"You know I have to get a job. I told you the school is closing. I can't marry without a job."

"Nonsense. Sell the forty to Atkins. You work too hard. Marry and farm Orin's place. You're stupid for a school-teacher. You said you were going to see the ocean. You could take Rosealee for a nice honeymoon to the ocean. Your father took me on a train to Wyoming. We saw Indians out there."

"I'll think about it.'

Joseph fidgeted in his chair. It was getting light and she turned off her bedlamp.

"Well I know you wanted to marry Rosealee when Orin did. Now you can. So do it." She closed her eyes, a clear signal for him to leave her alone with her pain which had deepened her lines and shrunk her face. Joseph kissed her forehead.

Jim Harrison: Farmer

54

One late sleepless night a week later he came downstairs and ate some herring alone. He tiptoed through the parlor and into the bedroom but his mother was sleeping, if fitfully. He missed the rye bread she made once a week. The rye bread was good with herring as was the salty butter she no longer churned. He looked down at his plate of herring and closed his eyes, overwhelming himself with the feeling that they were somehow all alive and vibrant again. Arlice was there teasing her older sisters to distraction. Dad would tell her to stop but he was gentlest to her. Dad himself was very happy because he had gotten a nickel more a bushel than he had expected for the potatoes. The pigs were fat, ready for their week of butchering, plus a single steer for the winter's beef. The beef was an event. They ate little fresh beef except right after butchering before it was dried, canned, or corned. That is why they so enjoyed Orin's or anyone else's venison, or the occasional gifts of beef from other farmers that were always reciprocated. It was hard to admit that you looked forward to a milk cow going old and dry. But you got tired of veal from the very young and utterly useless bulls that no one wanted to castrate and raise as beef. You might keep a single bull or three or four farmers would share one. In a way they were wild animals and everyone had stories of near misses after being chased by an angry bull. His sisters all giggled when they watched the bull mate outside the kitchen window. Dad sent them into the house but Joseph got to stay. The same

Jim Harrison: Farmer

55

when horses bred. Horses were more interesting Joseph thought. Pigs were the funniest.

But when he opened his eyes he was alone. His mother began whimpering in her sleep. He got out the whiskey and turned on the radio.

Jim Harrison: Farme

Everyone got disgusted with winter by March and usually before, and a major April storm could bring on a fit of sheer spite in anyone. Carl used to say that winter was like a cow chewing the same cud for six months or more. And despite all the church activities, school, the dances and card parties at the Grange Hall, everyone grew morbid and nervous toward spring, about ten degrees out of kilter in fact. There were more fights at the tavern than at any other time of year and the simplest family quarrels extended into days of silence with the snow and wind outside roaring louder than the wood fire in the stove. Spring, whether false or not, brought on laughter and a kind of easeful drowsiness, a time of general good feeling when people yawned and smelled the air with a few weeks' respite before the fields would be dry enough to plow. Joseph thought it a grand time; it was simply that they had all lived through another winter and that under its heavy lid of snow and ice and frozen ground the earth was actually alive.

For three days in April it became very warm. At school all the children took their sack lunches outside to eat. They became dreamy with the promise of spring and were inattentive. At recess the older students sat on an elm log out near the road and some of the boys took their shirts off. The younger students wallowed around in the sea of mud that was the schoolyard. The first polliwogs were caught from the swamp

Jim Harrison: Farmer

57

behind the school and stuck in Ball jars to be studied and die. In the fields there was a vague cast of green emerging beneath the brown matted grass. Joseph and Rosealee opened all the windows for the first time since October, letting the fresh air wipe away the musty fetor of the coal stove, varnished wood, chalkdust, the urine from the faulty toilets.

Joseph stood at the window and watched a group of boys playing marbles. It seemed sad that the best players won them all. One boy was much admired because his father owned a junkyard and supplied his son with small ball bearings that the boys called "steelies." They were much desired and though the boy from the junkyard was on the verge of being retarded and came from a bitterly poor family he had his place in the sun each spring with his steelies.

"How's your mother?" Rosealee came up behind and put an arm around Joseph's waist. When the children saw any sign of affection between them they shrieked and jumped around like young goats. Catherine walked by the window and pretended not to notice them.

"Bad. It can't last much longer." The pressure of her hand drew him to her. Since their night under the lights they had become rather wild-eyed. With two lovers Joseph's appetite increased. He had heard of the magic power of oysters but none were available in the area except canned ones that tasted like tin. The night before Joseph had roasted two grouse for himself and made some soup for his mother. After he had returned from a session with the new Rosealee, he had lazed in the bathtub then fried himself a steak which he ate while listening to the news and drinking his nightcap of bourbon with a little water.

"Do you want to go to the movies or something tonight?"

"I can't. I'd have to get someone to sit with mother. Charlotte's coming tomorrow, so we can go out then."

"I'll come over for a while." She insisted.

"Don't bother. I got to get some sleep. I'm going to spread manure tomorrow." He felt irritated with his runaround.

Jim Harrison: Farmer

"It's too warm and wet. You'll just get stuck."

"The news said it was going to freeze hard. I'll get up early."

"Damn, I wanted it to be nice for the weekend." Rosealee walked out into the foyer and rang the bell that ended recess. She had an impossible case of spring fever and wondered aloud why anyone lived so far north.

Joseph remained at the window as the children filed in, feeling weak and stupid with his lies. Now he would have to spread manure whether he wanted to or not. He walked from Rosealee's room through the door of the partition into the upper grades. There were only fifteen students left from a high of thirty some years back. The loss of students was easily explained by the number of empty, marginal farms in the township.

"Sit down. Shut up. Put your books away. Take out paper and pencil. We're going to have a quiz. We've studied Emily Dickinson for a week. The question is," Joseph went to the blackboard, "was Emily Dickinson lonely because she wrote those poems or did she write the poems because she was lonely. Use examples." There were groans. The question approached gibberish but Joseph wanted to sit and think. He had lied to Rosealee because Catherine was coming over to go riding after school and he no longer could face the two of them in a single day, for both physical and emotional reasons.

Some of the girls screamed. A garter snake was wriggling down an aisle toward his desk. The boys laughed.

"Robert, take the snake outside."

"I can't, sir. I'm frightened of snakes." Robert wore a red nylon jacket he had insisted Rosealee buy him. The jacket was exactly like the one James Dean wore in a recent movie. "How many examples do we have to use, sir?"

"Three," Joseph said. A girl stood on her desk seat as the snake passed. "Daniel, take the snake outside before I tie it around your ugly neck."

"Yes, sir." Daniel stumbled forward though Joseph knew

Jim Harrison: Farmer

---

he hadn't brought the snake in. He lacked that much imagination. He was a Pole, the son of war refugees, and had signed up for the Navy for the coming June. He wanted to fight Communism. His father talked about the evils of Communism in the tavern every afternoon and bored everyone silly. Daniel lifted the snake gently and dropped it out the window. He leaned far out the window with his fat butt jutting into the classroom. He was teased because he farted constantly. "It crawled under the building, sir."

"That's nice. Thank you, Daniel." Daniel returned to his desk and pulled out his American literature text book. He simply couldn't remember anything, so out of despair cheated on every test. Joseph didn't mind; he thought of Daniel as inane cannon fodder. When the Navy recruiter had called to inquire about his seniors Joseph had said there were only two boys and one was a sure thing. Joseph enjoyed talking to the Navy recruiter who it seemed had sailed the seven seas, though Joseph found he knew nothing of marine biology.

"Sir?" One of the girls had her arm raised.

"Yes, Susan." He wasn't getting much thinking done.

"Did Emily Dickinson ever have a boyfriend?" All the girls giggled.

"Not in the ordinary sense of the term. She wrote love letters to a man but I'm sure she died a virgin." The word "virgin" brought forth nervous laughter and a few of the boys slugged at each other and rolled their eyes wildly. "Cut the crap," Joseph added. He was a stern disciplinarian though he didn't mind the snake prank. He remembered stuffing a large blue racer in his own teacher's purse and zipping it back up. He was delighted when the teacher fainted at lunch hour. She had been a boring old nitwit and loved to hit her students with a maple ruler.

As the students wrote with a mixture of disinterest and puzzlement Joseph tried with a notable lack of success to clarify his thoughts. He was addicted to Catherine as the dope

Jim Harrison: Farmer

60

addicts he read about were addicted to their drugs. When he forced her from his mind the image of her body oozed in from a corner and he felt it in the pit of his stomach. He did not put much stock in psychologizing but knew from what he read that she was a classic neurotic. Sometimes her fingernails bled from her chewing. She was very pretty but sallow from refusing to eat well. Her alcoholic mother was a great burden to her and her father had been absent so much of the time she had no choice but to shoulder it. She clearly had decided on drama school because she knew that her only true gifts were for fantasy, for acting out parts that lessened the dreariness of the world. She sat through every change of movies with great enthusiasm and had managed to make friends with Robert, who often accompanied her. They made an odd and stagy pair for a country school, Joseph thought. He felt tremendously awkward when he and Rosealee met them at the movies. The month before they had all gone to a restaurant for hamburgers and Catherine had rubbed his leg under the table.

During the afternoon recess Joseph had glanced at the quiz papers. "Was Emily Dickinson lonely? Yes Emily Dickinson was lonely for we know she had no man friend while she lived. So she wrote verses. Who knows if she was married she would not have written these verses. That is the question that stumps us today." Joseph dropped all the papers in the wastebasket except Robert's and Catherine's but then theirs proved to be full of arch posturings. Robert insisted that the world was full of lonely, bored individuals. He didn't like "E. Dickinson" because she "didn't face up to reality." Catherine insisted that though the poetess didn't know "physical love," "she was one of the great lovers in all poetry along with Elizabeth Barrett Browning and the Brontë sisters." Over his many years of teaching Joseph had come to be suspicious of mere literacy when it was so ubiquitously devoted to idiocies, livestock reports, comics, and the sports page.

Jim Harrison: Farmer

When Joseph reached home after his drink at the tavern Catherine pulled into the driveway after him in her Jeep. She wore the same riding clothes she had worn their first day. Going riding had become a euphemism for their lovemaking, a perfect cover in an area where perfect covers were so impossible most lovers were forced into blatancy out of desperation. In seven months they hadn't managed to make love in a bed—they were limited to the barn, the granary, or the car. Catherine preferred the car while Joseph liked it least because of its vulnerability to surprise by strangers and the fact that his bad leg made him feel the most awkward in the car.

Joseph checked his mother while Catherine walked to the barn ostensibly to saddle her horse. A neighbor lady who spent the day with his mother had left a tuna fish casserole on the table with cooking instructions. Joseph dumped it in the garbage. Casseroles reminded him of all the dreadful local events that called for potluck—weddings, anniversaries, the gatherings of mourners after funerals.

When he walked into the stable it took a moment or two for his eyes to focus from the bright light of the afternoon. Catherine was sitting on her saddled horse, nude.

"Jeeesuss, Catherine!" he exploded.

"I'm Lady Godiva." She laughed and walked the horse past him. He grabbed the bridle.

Jim Harrison: Farmer

———

"Get off, you goddamn lunatic. What if somebody walked in?"

"What if they walked in anyway?" She slipped nimbly off the horse and stood facing him with her hands on her waist.

Of course she was right, Joseph thought. They moved past the stanchions to their blanket. "You just surprised me is all. I'm an old man. You got to watch my heart."

She began by doing what she called the "other thing." The week before during her period she did the other thing with great intensity and Joseph enjoyed it, never having done it with anyone else before. Catherine's versatility astounded him but he supposed it was only his own inexperience. They made love on their hands and knees then dozed off into a sweet spring haze.

"Hello Joe, what you doing?" It was the doctor looking over the stable partition.

"Napping." Joseph said, still dazed. Then he looked frantically beside him where Catherine gave out a moan with her jeans clutched over her face.

"I'll wait outside." The doctor waved and left.

"What are we going to do?" Catherine scrambled into her clothes while Joseph yawned and scratched his head.

"He won't say anything. I know him." He felt terribly embarrassed but the doctor was such an old friend that Joseph wasn't worried about their loss of secrecy.

Dr. Evans and Joseph sat on the porch as Catherine drove out of the yard. She beeped and waved.

"You ought to stick to fucking grownups, dumbass."

"Yes." Joseph knew he was due some advice.

"When they're as young as she is and that mixed up they'll make trouble for you. I treat her mother." The doctor sipped on his drink. "Of course you might want some trouble. You're sure enough going to get it. How long is this going on?"

"Since October. It was her idea."

Jim Harrison: Farmer

———

The doctor whistled and hooted. "You're forty-three and she's seventeen and it's her idea. You're cracking up, boy."

"How's Mother?" He drank deeply and stood to get another one.

"She won't last the month. Neither will you if the major finds out." The doctor laughed at the idea. "Of course he probably suspects what she's like. Maybe he'll just shoot you in your good leg." He laughed again. "She didn't actually look too bad especially for this county where they pork up so fast. You taking vitamins? Rosealee looks happy enough. Of course you know it will get out before long some way or another."

Joseph was flustered then belligerent. "If it's going to get out I may as well keep it up because it's fun and I sat on my ass too long."

"Don't get pissed off. I'm almost seventy and I still manage on the rare or not-so-rare occasion. My dad told me you don't regret the ones you do when you're old and thinking back, you only regret the ones you don't." The doctor slapped his leg and hooted. "How about another drink?"

Joseph took his glass. "You still want to go to Canada in June?"

"If you're not shot dead." The doctor followed him in and poked at some venison chops Joseph had thawing on the counter. "Can I stay for dinner?"

"Sure. That is, if you'll shut up about me getting shot."

They were both mildly drunk by the time they finished eating. The doctor was repeating a story Joseph had heard often but wasn't tired of, how the doctor had left Wales as a young man right after medical school. He had read some American sporting magazines and wanted to come to a country where hunting and fishing weren't more or less limited to the privileged few. So he emigrated to Canada but Canada lacked good brown-trout fishing so he had ended up in northern Michi-

Jim Harrison: Farmer

———

64

gan by the time of the First World War. He was promptly drafted but always said that he had done the best "to save my ass" so he could return to his fishing. The doctor despised the crudity of most American sportsmen and over the years had infected Joseph with many of his nineteenth-century attitudes, so Joseph was thought a bit strange by many other hunters and fishermen. The doctor released most of the fish he caught and limited his bag in grouse to what he thought any area could easily replace. The doctor's other *bête noire* was the medical profession. He was unpopular among other doctors because he strongly disapproved of their self-importance and fee gouging.

They went in to talk to Joseph's mother but she was sleeping fretfully. The doctor gave her a shot of morphine as a gift for a full night's sleep. Joseph poured a nightcap, dizzy from fatigue and whiskey. He was pleased not to have to face Rosealee at mid-evening.

"Catherine says that Robert's a homosexual," Joseph suddenly blurted out. He had meant to keep this secret.

"I know it." The doctor was diffident.

"How did you know?" Joseph was surprised.

"You can tell when you've been in the business. He's a good boy. He'll be OK."

Joseph was shocked at what little importance the doctor placed on his secret. "What can we do about it?"

"Nothing. You can start by leaving him alone. He'll probably move to the city where he can find some friends. So don't say much and don't let Rosealee say much. He's a man and it's his business and you can't change him. Some are and most aren't and it's always been like that."

"Well there aren't many up here," Joseph insisted.

"You'd be surprised. There's even some married men in town that are." The doctor began laughing. "There's even a doctor that is. But the best thing is to act normal with Robert. Life has tricked him or maybe it hasn't. Who's to say? I'm not going to. We got enough crazies, wife beaters, and drunks not

Jim Harrison: Farmer

65

to criticize queers, don't you think? Also enough bad marriages to drive this doctor up the wall and over the top. I've seen enough in my practice to not care who is fucking whom or what. Except if they get themselves shot." He laughed and stood patting Joseph on the head. "I'm sorry. I know I promised."

Joseph was pleased to know a man with so much composure. It put his mind at ease about Robert whom he disliked anyway. Joseph had been worried that Rosealee would be hurt but knew he himself hurt her over and over again. When she found out he'd have her talk to the doctor. Poor Rosealee with Orin dead and Robert so confused and me fooling with that girl. Joseph put his head on his arms among the venison bones and vowed with little conviction that he would straighten out his life.

Jim Harrison: Farmer

The thaw disappeared during the night and when Joseph walked into the barnyard at dawn the ground was hard again and an icy wind came straight down from the northwest. It was so cold the mud puddles were solid enough to walk on. The first load was already in the spreader so Joseph lit a cigarette while the tractor went through its faltering warm-up period which always seemed deafening at dawn. He watched the stars begin to disappear as he made several passes over their garden spot and was so intent on the stars he narrowly missed the grape trellis on his way out of the garden. He felt aimless in this chore. He had no intention of planting field corn but it would be equally aimless to waste the manure so he started into the field as the sky began to lighten.

Throughout the morning he was superheated while forking the manure onto the spreader and then freezing while he drove the tractor, but he knew he would be done by lunchtime. In the old days it was a week-long job but their last cow was gone by Christmas and Catherine's horse didn't amount to much. He remembered going into town with his father on Saturdays. Some town kids on the street taunted him by yelling that he smelled like cowshit and Joseph had poked one hard enough to discourage the others. Years later when he had gone to County Normal for a year to study to be a teacher the boy he had hit also attended and they became friends though the boy later disappeared in World War II at Monte Casino.

Jim Harrison: Farmer

67

On his last load Joseph became sure that he would be ill. The deepest manure was warm and gave off a gas and this, combined with a hangover and troubled stomach, made him nauseous. He was shivering by the last forkful despite his exertion. Other than a slight cold once a year Joseph was never ill. He prided himself on his constitution and his ability to virtually will himself away from sickness. Perhaps this was only an extension of his attitude toward his bad leg; from his ninth year he had simply chosen not to notice it, and any pain the leg gave him, any awkwardness or disability it caused, were to be thought of in no other terms but as facts of life. On the way toward the house from the barn he slipped on a patch of ice and swore. Hours before the metal blades of the spreader had flicked against his jacket cuff and he had had a chilling vision of his body without an arm.

In the house he washed up and warmed some soup for his mother. She lay propped up against two pillows with her Bible on her lap. Her eyes were open but at first she didn't notice him.

"Can I help you to the toilet?"

"No thanks. You don't look so good yourself." She smiled at him then her eyes rolled backward and her hands clutched and released. "It comes in waves," she said apologetically. "I had a fine sleep and good dreams. I dreamed when you were ten and shot the weasel that was after chickens. Such a little weasel to kill chickens. Then Arlice when she won the contest for being the prettiest at the fair and without a new dress."

"I think I just got a little flu. I'll have Rosealee come look after you and I'll go to bed."

"Don't bother. You know, Yoey, I heard you and Dr. Evans talking. I shouldn't say anything because I wasn't meant to hear it but you should marry Rosealee and stop messing with that girl. She comes over to ride and she never rides." Then she smiled and reached for his hand. "Of course all men have vinegar in them, even your father, but you are up in years to be fooling with such a young girl."

Jim Harrison: Farmer

"I know it. I'm a bad man but sometimes it's great fun to be bad." They both laughed and she squeezed his hand.

"You're a good man. If that made men bad we'd all be lost. I'm almost out of your way. You take Rosealee for a nice honeymoon trip. Maybe out to Wyoming, huh? There are mountains there."

When Joseph got into bed the chills descended on him so strongly he got up and filled a hot water bottle. He thought he wanted whiskey but the idea quickly nauseated him. He added two quilts and lay beneath their weight hugging the water bottle to his stomach. The strength had left his body and he felt like so much dead meat that somehow managed to ache in every muscle and joint. He slept fitfully then awoke with a start as the bottle slipped down against his member. He swore and turned on his stomach. The pain was so real it was oddly delicious and simple after so much mental torment over his mother, Catherine, and Rosealee. He had dreamed briefly of Rosealee when they were both fourteen at the party. *Where was Orin? Arlice and her boyfriend were in the barn. Rosealee was laughing with the glasses of beer they had sneaked off with, spilling most of it but then they had already drunk many glasses. They walked a few rows into the tall corn with a slight breeze rasping the stalks and leaves together. They giggled and drank their beer and began kissing kneeling there. She raised her dress some, not wanting to get it dirty. He had his hands on her thighs. She took his thing out saying she had never touched one before. Even in the cornfield the music was loud and people were shouting with the light of the bonfire against the stalk tips. He heard his mother's high full laugh. He raised Rosealee's dress higher and rubbed against her. The polka band began playing a slower tune, like a waltz. Rosealee moved her thighs together and he was trapped there. They kissed over and over* and then the warmth of the hot water bottle ended the dream.

Joseph wondered at the exactness of the dream and thought for a moment he smelled the cornstalks, beer, Rosealee's scent

Jim Harrison: Farmer

69

and heard the slow mournful music. Arlice had called and Rosealee slipped back away from him and the hard rub of her thighs had made him come onto the ground. Rosealee had said get up get up they'll find us and think we did something. Joseph smiled in his fever. It had been the most splendid night of his life but afterward Rosealee blushed when she saw him; then developed an interest in Orin who was even then his best friend. Joseph slept again but the dreams were bad and full of sick horses that had to be shot and buried out behind the granary.

When he awoke the room was black and the door closed. He was startled to hear someone in the kitchen. For a minute he lost his bearings completely and reached for his leg to see if it was covered with bandages as it had been thirty-five years ago. He heard again his mother scream *I can't stop the bleeding it won't stop bleeding. His father running from the field with him held in his arms. He was dazed and his pants were torn and his leg was hot and twisted. They were buzzing wood with a belt off the neighbor's tractor attached to the big saw and they gunned the tractor to cut a big log. He backed into the belt when he threw his dog a stick and before anyone could move the belt had gripped his pants toward the roller which mangled his leg, even ripped the skin from his crotch.* Now Joseph tossed his head on the pillow and yelled. He heard steps and the light came on.

"What's wrong?" Rosealee knelt beside him and he began weeping.

His fever broke on Sunday evening and he awoke drenched with sweat and asked Rosealee to make him some coffee with ice. Rosealee put on his overalls and boots to do the few chores; she normally had a hard time getting the geese back in the pen. The geese were suspicious of everyone but Joseph and his mother, and Rosealee had to chase them with a broom. When Rosealee stood at the end of the bed half-nude sorting his clothes he was swept back into his dream and again felt that incredible choked tenderness a fourteen-year-old in love feels. Her bottom was framed by the white iron rungs of the bed and she blushed as she turned and caught his stare.

"This summer let's go out in a cornfield and drink beer."

"Fine by me." She laughed. "Only I won't run away."

"I wish it was summer tonight." Joseph was wet and clammy. He wiped his brow with the sheet.

"You'd be too weak, silly. I'll make you some supper when I get through chores."

"Please turn off the light. I want to think."

Back in the dark Joseph almost regretted that his fever had passed. The fever was helping him sort his problems. Sickness often creates a space to live in, freeing the mind from the habitual if only for a day or two. Ordinary stresses disappear and when one returns to usual routines everything seems a bit more clear though sadly the clarity quickly passes. Joseph had lain all afternoon deep in the past, staring out his window at the bare orchard and the field beyond that; then came the wood lot where the creek ran through basswood and tag alder. After the accident his father had rigged small seats on the mowing machine and hay rake so Joseph could sit beside him. They followed the horses from so many cool mornings into hot afternoons when the hay chaff made it hard to breathe. During the cutting of the first hay, meadowlarks and killdeer would swoop and flit around as if crippled, trying to draw them away from their nests. A few times they crawled around on the ground and found the nests with their pale smallish eggs. Then they would cut around the spot. Later when they got a tractor Joseph wore a brace so his left foot could work the clutch. He had never been able to handle the horses. You had to dig in with your heels and pull back hard to turn them, especially in the morning when they were well-rested and frisky. Plowing was also out of the question. Until they had managed to buy a tractor plowing was the most arduous work on the farm.

Jim Harrison: Farmer

———

Walking behind the horses you had to hold the handles steady, rein the horses, and twist the single blade unit around on corners, all with one foot walking in the furrow and the other on solid ground. Joseph agonized over this because his father became brutally tired during plowing. He learned years later that it was Dr. Evans that loaned his father the money for the tractor. Unfortunately his father was mystified by motors and could never keep the John Deere in good running order. The same was true with their used Model T, no matter how elementary the problem was. He would sit at the kitchen table in the evening listening to the radio and scratching his head over the owner's manuals for both tractor and car. Joseph would sit beside him and stare at the diagrams mournfully.

"I think we got a problem, Yoey."

"We'll figure it out, papa."

Only the fact that the neighbor boy was a good mechanic saved them. Joseph had smiled in his fever over the many times they had stood looking at the broken-down machinery and had decided to go fishing. His mother would pack sandwiches and a jug of lemonade and they would either go back to the beaver pond on state land and fish for brook trout or, if the car was working, drive to a small lake down the road where they would fish for bluegills and sunfish with long cane poles and bobbers. They would get back by dark and his mother and sisters would fry the fish in butter after dusting them with flour, salt, and pepper. They always ate the fish with brown bread and a simple cabbage salad with vinegar. Everyone was methodical and silent as they picked the bones, listening to the music on the radio, the air dense with the smell of fish fried in butter, the noise of frogs and night birds and crickets coming in from the screen door where June bugs often hung to the tiny-meshed wire. Then he and his sisters would wash up and kiss their parents and go upstairs where Joseph had a small room and the four girls slept in the other bedroom, though Arlice often came in and they would talk half the night

Jim Harrison: Farmer

---

about all the places Richard Halliburton had been in those books.

But by the time Arlice was thirteen and had her first period she stopped visiting him at night and he missed hearing about her secrets. Arlice's breasts became finer than her older sisters' and she wasn't heavy at all so they became a little jealous. One night when they were fifteen and his parents had gone to town Arlice showed him her breasts which he had peeked in and seen anyway years before, but they both became embarrassed. His sisters caught him peeking and told Mother who told Dad who took him out to the barn for a paddling. His father said yell, I'm not going to paddle you but it's not proper to peek at your sisters. When you grow up more in a few years you will understand.

In the eighth grade some of his friends made love to a homely fat girl but Orin said it wasn't so much fun. All the girls in school even the older ones liked Orin. He was the best at everything but hung around Joseph's house all the time because his home wasn't happy and besides Rosealee was there so much. Her father trapped for furs in the winter and she sometimes stayed for months, with her father giving them some money for her board before he drank it all up downstate where he would go to have some fun. Carl didn't want to take the money even though they were bitterly poor then but Rosealee's father just said he would drink it up anyway. Rosealee upset Joseph so much that he spent as much time as possible doing the chores and hunting after school with Orin. His leg though twisted had toughened to the point that he could hobble for hours on his brace. He worried that it would prevent him from becoming as tall as his father who was an even six feet but Joseph's growth stopped only an inch short. His chest was wide and his arms big partly because he compensated for his bad leg by using them more. When they pitched hay he would scramble around on his knees stacking it and when they pitched it into the mow he would always be there to spread and

Jim Harrison: Farmer

73

stack it. He also stayed on the wagon to arrange the crates of potatoes. The same when they unloaded them. So he ended up handling all the weight everyone else together handled. By fourteen when he and Orin and Arlice played Tarzan of the Apes in the barn, Joseph could climb the hay ropes hand over hand and then down the barn rafters hand over hand. It was good for him to become strong because it ended any teasing at school. They could always run from him but the time would always come when he could get hold of them if Orin hadn't first interceded. Orin hated farming even then. He only wanted to hunt and read about airplanes. When Orin was only eight his father had bought him a ride from some barnstormers at the fair and that had changed Orin's life and finally killed him.

Once late in the afternoon Joseph was ashamed to find himself weeping. For two years in the mid-twenties there had been a drought which left the corn shrunken and useless and blight had rotted the potatoes. Even the pigs grew thin from short rations. It looked like the bank would foreclose. At the fair Joseph had lost his two quarters and there was nothing to replace them with so he walked around the fair pretending he had lost his money playing horseshoes which he was good at. He later learned that Dr. Evans had saved the farm. Dr. Evans would look for any excuse to stop by with a big chunk of beef and a bottle of whiskey or case of beer. Once he said it was his birthday and that made them all happy as they ate but then Arlice piped in and said you had a birthday two months ago and his mother ran from the table.

Of course the discomfort and pain of poverty was more generalized than sharp. It was more difficult for the older girls who were in high school during the worst of the times. They were farmed out as servant girls to wealthier families in the county seat and in exchange for their work they were given room and board and a chance to go to high school. By the time Joseph and Arlice were to enter ninth grade the country school down the road had expanded into the higher grades. Joseph

Jim Harrison: Farmer

was happy, not wanting to expose himself to the possible cruelties of a new life. Arlice didn't mind; she was a happy girl who spent her free time day-dreaming and reading romantic novels far in advance of her age. And she saw how unhappy with envy the older girls were; they had moved into town when there was no money left to give them anything more than the clothing on their backs and not much of that. The whole family had been surprised when the girls kept themselves near or at the top of their classes. Joseph's father made much of the fact that though they were poor they weren't dumb. So much of the cruelty of poverty rests in the idea that it makes its victims feel unworthy, shy, willing to be pushed around by virtue of this economic accident.

Joseph remembered when a new fifty-cent oilcloth for their supper table was an event. He and Arlice would stand by the table and admire the small squares of roses printed on it. He also remembered that his mother waited until after supper, when everyone was seated quietly in the living room, to open her package from Montgomery Ward that contained a new iron skillet. They all jumped around laughing when the parcel also contained a new nightgown his father had added to the order. Perhaps the bitterest memory was the two months when the radio broke and they had no means to fix it. Everyone walked around pretending it didn't exist, that something other than a radio sat on the dresser. Finally the neighbor boy who was always being called upon to poke at their machinery traced the problem to a twenty-cent tube that was burned out and easily repiaced. He was amazed at their stupidity in such matters.

In his fever Joseph had made a tentative decision to begin farming again. He knew it might dissipate but his resolve increased with good memories of the years immediately before the Depression. After the blight and drought there had been four years of bumper crops and a general feeling of ease and relief. It meant new dresses after harvest for his mother and the girls, and often a new fishing pole for Joseph. He was over-

Jim Harrison: Farmer

whelmed on his twelfth birthday when Dr. Evans had dropped off an Ithaca twenty-gauge shotgun. It meant that he no longer had to try to pot grouse on the ground with his old .22; he could shoot them on the wing like his father and the doctor though his father much preferred the meat hunter's favorite, the rabbit. During the bleakest fall the doctor and his father had killed two large deer. The antlers still hung in the granary. They ate themselves silly on the venison and in the week that followed the children were often allowed a glass of the foul-tasting but potent homemade wine. Joseph laughed when he thought that his father's homemade wine had forever ruined wine drinking for him. He and Orin had once drunk it in great gulps from a jug only to spend hours out in the woodlot vomiting in secrecy.

He heard Rosealee come through the pump shed and into the kitchen. Then his light was on and he raised an arm across his eyes.

"I hate your geese. One bit my leg. What do you want for supper?" She was flushed and her knees were muddy.

"There's some soup. I got to take a bath first." He swung his legs from the bed and the weakness returned.

"Look, I'll take your classes tomorrow. You rest, or you can wait and call me in the morning." She slipped the overall straps from her shoulders. Joseph grabbed at her when she leaned for her skirt. "Take your bath first. You must have been dreaming about someone else." She rather liked it on the odd occasion Joseph was ill. At one time she had dreamed of being a nurse; as a girl every Sunday morning she had nursed her father back from his monumental hangovers. But then in her teens he had managed to get a bleeding ulcer and neglected to see a doctor; she could not nurse him back and he died a few days before she graduated from high school.

Joseph lazed in his bath thinking how both poverty and wealth were mischievous: Keats was poor and Byron rich and

Jim Harrison: Farmer

neither had the edge. Walt Whitman whom Joseph revered was neither poor nor rich if you could believe what the man said and that seemed to give him an edge over writers who thought about it all the time. The week before on Friday Joseph had read from *Leaves of Grass* and Robert had objected on the grounds that Whitman was "sentimental." Joseph had called him a goddamn fool and nitwit who read only science fiction bullshit. The students had loved this show of temper and Robert had walked angrily out of the schoolhouse. Then Catherine interjected that everyone couldn't like the same writers and he had replied that some were dumb and some were bright. The squabble had anyway ruined the afternoon for poetry so Joseph administered a geometry quiz that drove him silly with its tediousness. Only Daniel scored a hundred percent and as always he copied the answers directly from the book.

"Your soup stinks." Rosealee was standing at the door. The soup was made out of cabbage and venison marrow bones and could be smelled through the steam rising from the tub.

"Tough shit. Don't eat it. Why don't you get in the tub?" He reached for her and she slammed the door.

His day and a half of fever had sharpened his interest in Rosealee. He frequently dreamed of her anyway but his sickness had cast the dreams in a pleasanter more sexual light. Conversely his thoughts of Catherine turned sour and he wondered how he could have been so stupid as to get involved with her. Life was so sudden in its impositions. First Mother was well and then she was going to die. One day his father had fished and on the afternoon of the next day he was pulled from the river dead. The first morning of school the fall before a pretty girl in a yellow skirt had stared at him with her hazel eyes and when she turned to introduce herself to the class her skirt pulled upward and he saw her legs were lovely. Her speech was southern but not trashy. She read books and announced to him she loved classical music. They often chatted

Jim Harrison: Farmer

——————

77

after school and he was delighted that so bright a student would grace his last year for he already knew the school would close and he had no intention of teaching in town. She was slender and her hair was dark brown. When a farm girl was bright she did not presume to make it known other than by shyly turning in good work. Catherine, however, was outspoken. She could even hit a softball and shoot baskets with the boys who were all smitten by her though none dared ask her out. After their October day passed Joseph realized that he had been thinking about making love to her since the first day of school. But as winter lengthened her instabilities became more obvious; she grew fretful and restless after the novelty of country life wore thin. The Christmas vacation had brightened her again but this new energy soon dissipated and she became more demanding of Joseph, even to the point of discussing marriage which he refused to think about. He could not imagine her camping by the ocean with him. She had no interest in his fishing or hunting; no interest in rivers and lakes and oceans.

Jim Harrison: Farmer

They sat through the evening on the front porch. May had been cold and rainy but now in the middle of the month it had finally become warm and maple pods dropped from the trees like pale green grasshoppers. Mint sprouted in the ditch along the road and the first of the lilacs began to appear. Joseph's mother lay back in the porch swing, too weak to move herself. Only her eyes, which were clear blue and liquid, moved. She had not spoken for over an hour. Joseph felt choked, constricted. He suspected that it was the last time they'd sit on the porch together. He held his hands over his face peeking through the cracks in his fingers at the honeysuckle with its overwhelming odor. A car passed on the gravel road with stones rattling around under its fenders. The car beeped. Joseph did not look up to see which neighbor it was.

"I'm tired," his mother announced.

"I'll carry you in." Joseph stood and moved to the side of the swing.

"I mean tired of this," she waved at her body. "It's worse than having a baby every day." She smiled at the thought. "I'm not alive for months now. Your father never taught me to shoot a gun." She smiled again at the thought.

"I'll call the doctor and see what he thinks."

"I know what he thinks. Take me in now."

They paused, hearing their first whippoorwill of the year.

Jim Harrison: Farmer

79

The whippoorwill reminded Joseph of trout fishing which he had done none of this spring because of his mother's illness.

Later, after he had carried his mother into the house and given her her pills he called the doctor. Her eyes were squeezed tight with pain and Joseph became wordlessly angry. He often found himself wandering around the house or barnyard muttering goddamn god. The doctor was agreeable to meeting him at the tavern so he told his mother he'd be back in an hour. She stared at him in the doorway. Then waved him away.

The last of the light disappeared on the way to the tavern. It was still warm and bugs splattered against the windshield. He stopped for a moment in the swamp and after a wary pause the peepers were deafening. He was embarrassed because his thoughts drifted from his mother's pain to trout fishing. The cancer had been diagnosed after Christmas and considering that she was in her mid-seventies the doctor predicted she would last only three months or so. His sisters all came for long visits until he was as sick of them as his mother was of the cancer. He finally asked them to stop coming until what he called the "final days." Arlice even came way out from New York. They had spent a good week talking and drinking.

The doctor's car was the only one in the parking lot and he stood when Joseph entered.

"She's bad?"

"Terrible. I thought you said she'd die by now."

"I'm not God."

Joseph laughed. The doctor was famous for his brusqueness and lost many patients to the newer doctors who were more tactful with their fat, sedentary patients. The doctor retained only the farm farmilies who tended to call him when they were truly ill.

The bartender brought them a succession of bourbons and glasses of beer, returning to the radio at the end of the bar where he listened to the Detroit Tigers game. He had been lis-

Jim Harrison: Farmer

tening to the Tigers games since Joseph was a little boy, it seemed.

"We should be fishing tonight. George got a four-pound brown on the Pine the other night. Mayflies are thick."

"Sure," Joseph said, "I could set fire to the house, then go fishing. I thought of drowning her the other night. I sometimes wake up and can hear her weeping."

"It's gone on long enough." The doctor looked at Joseph for a hint of recognition. He got it immediately. And that released them to talk of trout and the number of drumming grouse they had heard which would mean a good season in October.

Back at the house the doctor told him to stay in the kitchen. He disappeared into the bedroom with his bag, then reappeared within a few minutes looking pale and distracted. Then Joseph went in and kissed his mother good-bye. Her face was lax, the eyes already closed.

"Thank you." Joseph said returning to the kitchen.

"Call in the morning." The doctor finished his drink and they shook hands.

Joseph spent the night seated beside her bed. He turned off all the lights in the house and took a bottle and glass into the bedroom. Three times during the night he felt her forehead as it gradually cooled toward room temperature. The night was dark and moonless and he couldn't see her on the bed until toward morning when the wind came up followed by a brief thunderstorm. Then he could see her during the flashes of lightning and even the frogs grew quiet in the thunder that followed. He felt irritated that he had waited so long to force the issue. There were no miracles in such cases. Now she only looked as if she were sleeping the sleep she had deserved months before. Throughout the night his grief changed to intermittent anger, relaxed into fine memories, became swollen and overwhelming, subsiding near dawn into bleak self-pity,

Jim Harrison: Farmer

81

an emotion he had never allowed himself. After his leg had been ruined Joseph's father had taught him never to pity himself. Such pity only further weakened a person, made one vulnerable to an essentially pitiless world. Thus no one in the family ever complained of anything except in the most extreme circumstance. His father who had been a hard drinker might loudly announce a hangover at breakfast but the statement was full of vigor and some humor. He often referred to himself as dumbass. When a horse crushed his toes so that the nails came off he was silent. He hobbled along as Joseph had hobbled since his eighth year, arrogant but full of laughter.

At dawn Joseph spent some time wondering if he should draw the sheet up over her face. He cooked himself three eggs and forgot to eat them. The rooster crowed incessantly. He laughed when he remembered a rooster years ago that crowed through the night and his father had been so irritated he had chased it around in the dark without catching it. He had come back in and got Joseph's .22 and asked him to hold the flashlight so he could shoot the bastard. They had fried chicken for breakfast and were very happy, fried chicken being a treat reserved for Sundays and special occasions.

As it became daylight Joseph thought of calling his sisters but decided to wait. He planned to say "she's dead" and hang up except with Arlice in New York whom he would ask not to come unless she truly wanted to. There was no point in her coming over a thousand miles to see a dead body. Joseph drew the sheet up over her face. Her hair was a rich brown with only a little gray. The hair looked the same but her face had begun to darken.

Joseph called the doctor.

"You didn't have to call so early," the doctor said.

Jim Harrison: Farmer

———

82

*A*t one time from a distance you would see a man behind a single-bladed plow and a team of horses. Behind the man a boy stumbled along the uneven furrow picking up earthworms. When the boy filled a can with worms he would dump the contents of the can into a larger pail in the middle of the field. In the pail the worms had a bedding of soil, damp peat moss, and coffee grounds to keep them vigorous. At the end of the day after the horses were unharnessed, rubbed, and fed, the father and the boy would look at the worms and try to decide if they had enough for a three-day fishing trip they planned after the spring plowing.

"Do we have enough, Yoey?"

"Maybe almost." The boy stuck his hand deep in the pail.

Then they would walk in to supper. Sometimes the father would offer his arm as if flexing his muscle and the boy would hang onto the arm like a monkey until they crossed the barnyard and reached the house. Then the boy would drop to his feet and scoot in the back door through the pump shed and announce to his waiting mother and sisters, "Dad wants his supper."

Jim Harrison: Farmer

One late afternoon Joseph heard a car and watched through the kitchen window as Rosealee got out and walked resolutely toward the house. He was mystified. She bore no cakes, pies, or casseroles and her face looked cloudy. He had seen her only a few hours before at school and she seemed happy enough then.

"I know," she said, looking stricken. Her face squeezed in pain and she began to weep.

"Know what?" But Joseph knew.

"Catherine. Why?"

Joseph looked down at his fishing tackle spread on the table. He fondled a fly called a Paramachene Belle. He loved its name though he never had taken any good fish with it. His brain began to whirl with false excuses.

"How do you know?" he asked lamely.

She sat down across from him as if collapsing. Her weeping was dry and intense. Joseph's thoughts turned to funerals where people's grief was so deep they seemed to wail rather than weep.

"I thought we had got so much better after that night." She faced him directly and his eyes lowered again to his fishing flies. She handed him a note. It was a sympathy card for his mother's death from Catherine and he cringed at the phrase "I know I can make you happy." Rosealee was helping him acknowledge the cards. Joseph's eyes closed and he saw

Rosealee's back raising his weight, her spine twisting the better to get at him.

"We are better. She's just a silly kid." His voice was tight and "kid" emerged so weak as to be barely susceptible.

"Then why are you fucking a kid? Why are you doing it? Aren't I enough? I've given my life to you."

"I figured I had some catching up to do, you know? I mean I haven't made love much in my life." The tightness was gone now and he felt his face flush with blood. He wanted to slip through one of the black cracks in the linoleum, into some sort of gap in existence far from either Catherine or Rosealee.

"Oh god. You sat here thinking and messed up your life and now I pay for it." She began crying again. "I'm not going to get another chance."

Joseph studied another fly intently. He wanted desperately to get rid of the ozone in the air and searched in panic for a single idea that might lift them both out of this horror.

"Oh goddamn you I hope you die." Rosealee tipped the kitchen table over in his lap, scattering the hundreds of trout flies on him and on the floor around his chair. She ran out of the house and he followed stumbling through the pump shed. He reached the car just as she turned around and was heading out of the driveway. Joseph waved but then had to dodge to avoid being run over.

He walked out back and fed the geese. They waddled toward him honking as he threw the corn. He felt giddy and was overwhelmed by the same emotions he had felt when he had lost Rosealee to Orin at fourteen. He suddenly wanted to strangle Catherine or, better yet, strangle himself. The mosquitoes from the pond clouded around his head and he did not have the presence of mind to brush them away. He wanted to somehow make his life simple again but was brought up sharply by the idea that it had never been very simple; he had merely neglected to do any of the things that most people occupy themselves with—marriage, children, bringing up a family,

Jim Harrison: Farmer
———
85

farming on your own. He had a simply gone through the easy motions of teaching and, other than that, read, hunted, and fished, mostly by himself. He had strung Rosealee along until it was too late for her to have the other child she wanted. And he had sat and talked with his mother for ten years about the past which she had begun to live in the day her husband died. The three geese looked up at him, with the last of the evening sun glowing off their white breasts. They honked and Joseph threw the rest of the corn.

Back in the kitchen he knelt and began gathering and sorting his trout flies. He stood in terror. Being that close to the floor took him back to when he was very young. The kitchen was the same and beneath the table top he saw the old iron stove and the woodbox in a new way, and the black iron body of the milk separator that he used to press his cheek against on hot days because the iron stayed cool. He squeezed his hands forgetting that they held the flies and several buried their points into his palms but, luckily, none past the barb. He took his flyrod from the corner and walked out through the pump shed and across the barnyard and through the gate. He was at the far end of the pasture near the fence that bordered the state land before it occurred to him that he had forgotten the brace he needed for long walking. He sat down on the rock pile and tears began to come but he pushed them back by swearing. His leg began to hurt from the pounding he had given it in his witless striding across the pasture. He lay down in the grass and closed his eyes, hearing a whippoorwill, then a nighthawk whirring just above him. The mosquitoes were dense around him so he got up and walked slowly back toward the house. It seemed that he had lost all of the spirit that he had maintained so steadily for so many years, that he had become a sack of willess meat and guts and bone like everyone else he scorned.

At the gate a car pulled into the yard in the gathering dark and the lights passed above him as he ducked. It wasn't Rosealee. Catherine knocked at the back door then began walking toward the barn. Joseph shrunk himself into a shadow. She must have driven past Rosealee's and, not seeing his car, assumed it was safe to come over. Joseph had no idea why he was hiding. Catherine turned on the light in the stable and leaned against a stanchion and began singing softly. She rubbed her horse's ears and looked around distractedly. She went to the door and called his name, then turned out the lights and left the barn. Joseph began breathing again when she drove out of the yard. For a moment looking through the dirty, fly-spattered barn window he had wanted her but that quickly passed into the absurd notion that he was watching a movie of Catherine and that any minute he himself might answer her call from the house or granary. The heat lightning he had seen in the pasture turned into a light, sprinkling rain, then into a downpour. Joseph sat near the gate on a large rock that they had hauled out of the field after chipping the plow blade. As they had unearthed it the boulder had turned out to be much larger than expected though the horses had had no difficulty with it. Joseph was soaked but it was a warm rain and he began to think the rain was cleansing his thoughts of their confusion and indecision. He knew he should go to Rosealee and ask forgiveness but the sight of Catherine was maddening and he wanted to be with her a few more times before he stopped it. He was gripping the flyrod so hard his hand had become sore.

In the kitchen Joseph poured himself his first large glass of whiskey after some self-congratulatory weeks of light drinking. He downed it in two gulps and sat waiting for his sureness to return. Maybe he would marry Rosealee, eat a little crow, and begin farming. It was too late for this year but he could get everything ready for the next. He was immediately reminded of what it would be like to sit on a tractor and cultivate two hundred acres of corn or soybeans, not to speak of plowing and disking it in the first place in single operations. What bleakness. A sea of corn was not the sea. Fuck Rosealee. If she wanted him they would at least take a long trip to see the

Jim Harrison: Farmer

———

87

ocean. He poured another drink and it occurred to him he was sopping wet so he shed his clothes and sat there drinking naked. He turned on the radio and heard a country singer wailing about a "cold, cold, heart," and Joseph saw his heart brittle and frozen in a meat locker. Then the heart became disturbingly airborne behind the lids of his closed eyes. The heart flushed like a blood-red grouse rocketing around the room. He felt if he had any courage he would keep his eyes closed and see what happened to his winged heart. He drank again deeply and some of the whiskey trickled down his chin and onto his chest. He heard a car pull up but he refused to open his eyes. Perhaps it was Rosealee and they could have their Friday night like they always had. There were footsteps in the room. For an idle moment he thought she might see his red heart.

"Joseph!" It was Catherine again. He might have known when the car drove behind the house where it could be hidden. "What are you doing? Jesus. Are you drunk?"

"Rosealee knows." He waited but she said nothing. She put her hand on his shoulder.

"Should we make love? I'm sorry. She had to know sooner or later."

"Why?" His eyes were still closed.

"I want to marry you," she said shyly.

"Will you cut that marriage shit?" Joseph exploded. His eyes opened as she burst into tears and hugged him. He drew her down on his lap. "I'm not going to marry anyone right now. I love you but I love Rosealee. I'm not sure what to do." He was stuttering.

"I won't mention it again." She stood and quickly slipped out of her clothes. They had never made love in the house before and somewhere in her head maybe she thought that might bring her closer to ownership.

Joseph was in the tavern by midnight. His lovemaking with Catherine had been dismal and she wept after he demanded

Jim Harrison: Farmer

88

that she stop cooing a popular song. And on the couch he was sure he felt the presence of ghosts; his mother gliding soundlessly through the room and his father telling him to slop the hogs. Catherine left in tears forgetting to put on her panties. Joseph poured another whiskey and held the panties up to the light with one hand. They were lovely; pale blue with a slight fringe of lace. He could see the lightbulb clearly through them and he felt silly. Jesus. He longed for a time not eight months back when sex was a regular pleasurable occasion with Rosealee, twice a week at the most. Now he had blown the lid off the well and had even managed to trip in the river while wading and thinking about Catherine's ass. One afternoon she had blown him as he was driving on a log trail in the woods and he had narrowly missed a tree. He smiled, though, when he thought how the superintendent would have reacted to his behavior. A fellow schoolteacher at another country school had been fired for "moral turpitude" but that was with boys. The men in the tavern had made much of the event. Daniel's father had yelled about "Commie cocksucker teachers" until Joseph told him to shut up or get thrashed.

Joseph joined a pinochle game when one of the partners dropped out. There were two farmers and a burly carpenter who tended to cheat even though they only played for quarters. He was often caught and embarrassed but couldn't resist slipping a card or two. It mystified everyone in the tavern as the carpenter was otherwise honest and hard working. The two farmers were dairymen who had been close to his father.

"And hello, Yoey," said one dairyman. "My cards have been shit but we can beat these morons."

"Hello, Einar. I'll play if you don't talk politics. And you can't talk about cattle, especially the heifers you keep for fun."

They all laughed, bestiality being a rather common joke. Usually they argued about farm prices or Eisenhower, who "got us out of Korea." The biggest source of argument ever

Jim Harrison: Farmer

89

was Truman's firing of MacArthur—there had been fights over that one. Joseph McCarthy had been dismissed as an "Irishman" by all but the Pole, Daniel's father, who revered him.

"Be the best you ever had. Never met a Swede who hadn't screwed a cow." Einar was Danish.

"You guys are so old you can't screw nothing. Deal the cards." The carpenter was in his twenties and featured himself a stud though it was commonly agreed that his exploits were totally invented.

"Yoey, when you going to marry Rosealee?" asked Nelse, the other dairyman. He was a shrewd Swede, quite rich in fact. He had been playing pinochle on Friday nights since Joseph could remember. Nelse had tried to help Joseph's father but quickly despaired, advising that Carl go back to the fishing boats like his people.

"I'll marry her when she gets ten years younger." More laughter.

After a few games the dairymen quit and Joseph, now dizzy with his succession of shots and beers, moved to the bar with the carpenter.

"If I was you I'd be screwing some of them junior and senior girls. Christ if I knew in school what I knew now I'd be screwing all the time."

Joseph looked away to hide his flush. Does he know? Probably not. The carpenter was an improbable big mouth whose brain was fixed on sex to the degree that it scarcely existed in his life. He would drive a hundred-fifty miles with some friends to a black whorehouse in Grand Rapids, returning with mythical screws that had been the agreed-upon stories in the car on the way back.

"Sixteen will get you twenty. You know that." He meant a sixteen-year-old equaled statutory rape which could net the offender twenty years. Up in this country where girls married as early as fifteen it never happened. Once when depressed with his students Joseph had decided that all country people were

Jim Harrison: Farmer

essentially hillbillies, no matter the distance to the Mason-Dixon line.

"I got to take the chance. You can't fuck when you're dead." The carpenter guffawed and Joseph moved down the bar to get the attention of the tavern owner long enough to get another drink.

"I'll have a double this time, Ted."

"What's wrong with you? Where's Rosie tonight?" All the older men in the area considered Rosealee a great beauty and couldn't comprehend why Joseph wouldn't marry her. "Doc was in early. He says you was going to fish the Pine tomorrow."

Now the power of the whiskey was in Joseph and he felt stupidly sentimental. He played some songs on the jukebox and the bartender looked askance at him because Joseph normally despised the jukebox. Then Joseph got up abruptly, spilling his beer, but his double was in his hand. He was going to stop and apologize to Rosealee.

Joseph drove into Rosealee's yard and noticed that the kitchen light was on. He pounded on the door and Robert appeared in pajamas.

"Mother doesn't want to see you," Robert said primly.

"Why?" Joseph began to push Robert aside.

"We both know. Catherine tells me everything. I don't see how you could do this to Mom after all these years."

Joseph shoved Robert aside and moved into the kitchen. Though it was nearly two a.m. Rosealee sat at her sewing machine in the corner.

"Please go away, Joseph. Let me think." Her face was ashen and she looked at the wall as she spoke.

"I just wanted to say. . ." Joseph stumbled against a chair.

"Please go away." She faced him. "I don't want to see you, Joseph. Maybe next week we can talk it over."

Joseph walked into the living room, lay down, and went to sleep.

Jim Harrison: Farmer

91

It seemed the doctor wanted to go fishing. He shook Joseph. Joseph rolled over in the midst of a dream in which he was being shaken by his father for netting spawning trout. *Orin did it Orin did it. There was a gunny sack full. His father said you kill all the mothers of trout and fishing will be bad for years. They ate them anyway.* The doctor said Yoey for christ's sake get up. Rosealee stood there arms folded when he opened his eyes. And Robert in his red jacket; Orin's mother cronelike peering from the corner. He swung his feet to the floor and drank tepid coffee, staring at his shoes, his head an air hammer. Robert walked away and so did Rosealee, looking older.

"Shame on you, Yoey," said Orin's mother. The doctor gestured her away and they stumbled out.

"You weren't at home but all the lights were on so I figured you would be down here." The doctor was cheery in the mid-morning light. They had meant to leave at dawn. "I overslept too, had a delivery. Let's go get your stuff." The doctor poked in his case in the back seat and handed Joseph a pill. "Here, take this and you'll survive."

They drove toward Tustin, an hour away, where the Pine River swept through a big swamp before entering a country of high clay banks. When they had the whole weekend they would drive farther north to the Manistee near Sharon, or farther yet up near Gaylord where there were three good rivers, the Pigeon, the Sturgeon, and the Black. A few weeks before Joseph had driven to the Pine with his seniors to bird-watch: what the superintendent had urged as "field trips." But when they reached the spot and Joseph had taken the Audubon packet from the trunk he found that Audubon had sent cards of shorebirds from the southeast. He sat on the trunk looking at beautiful pictures of roseate spoonbills, grebes, egrets, and pelicans while the kids played in the creek. But he had a Peterson Field Guide in the glove compartment and sent them off with it while he dozed in a glade. Robert and Catherine were tired of birds, and Daniel stayed in form by identifying robins as bluebirds. Lisa was a chippy cheerleader type who cracked gum and scarcely could read. A poor overweight girl named Karen rounded out the class. She was painfully shy but excelled at bird-watching. At first Joseph thought she was cheating but one day he walked with her and discovered that she even knew dozens of warblers on sight. She said there was a large swamp behind their barn and she had been doing her Audubon cards since the second grade when Rosealee had first given them to her.

When they came over a hill and stopped for gas they both noticed a bank of dark clouds on the horizon to the north.

"Oh pig shit," said the doctor.

"We're in trouble." Joseph's hangover had quickly lifted and he felt energetic. "What was that pill you gave me?"

"That's for fat sluggish women who want to diet and can't stay out of the icebox. Dexedrine." The doctor stared at the horizon. "We might get screwed out of our fishing and I've been thinking about it all week. Pisswilly."

"We might get there before it breaks," Joseph said without conviction.

They continued driving north through country not unlike the state land behind Joseph's farm: the spill from a moraine, glacial detritus which after the first wave of lumbering that scalped the land of its giant white pine had not been able to

Jim Harrison: Farmer

93

support anything but poplar, scrub oak, mixed stunted conifers, except in the richer swampy areas. The good farms in the county tended to follow a rather narrow irregular strip the glaciers had missed and their woodlots were dotted with huge beech and maple and the soil was rich. Joseph's father had stupidly chosen a fringe because of its beauty; all the improvident farmers in the county held one thing in common—they squatted on the moraine like hopeless ducks trying to scratch a living off the few inches of top soil that hovered over the pecker sand and gravel like a thin lid. But the rivers that ran swift and clean through this hilly country and the swamps in the valleys promised wonderful trout fishing, and Joseph and the doctor both loved this land the agriculturists thought of as useless.

They reached the river and were tying on leaders just as the sky unloaded with great streaks of lightning and hollow crackling thunder.

"Goddamn you," the doctor shook his fist at the sky.

"We've been had." Joseph reflected glumly that if he had been ready an hour earlier and not slept drunkenly on Rosealee's couch they would have picked up on the fine fishing that usually preceded a warm spring storm. He suspected the doctor was thinking the same thing.

They sat in the car drinking coffee from a thermos into which the doctor had poured several ounces of whiskey. Then he shook the thermos to mix it and poured a little extra whiskey into their tin cups. The fumes upset Joseph's stomach but he felt so jittery and light-headed from the pill he drank anyway. The storm was violent and it was nearly dark in the car; they could hear the treetops thrashing in the wind and lightning would light up their faces, then Joseph would start with the ensuing splitting crack of thunder.

"The river's going to turn brown. This is a cloudburst," he said obviously.

"Don't see why God can't give a fine doctor like me a day

off." He drank and paused. "Rosealee was sure pissed at you this morning. We sat at the dining room table drinking coffee and talking about it and watching you snore like a goddamn ape." He laughed and drank again. "Then we saw Orin's mother was in the kitchen hearing everything with Robert. When I said you would get over it and Catherine was just bored and horny Robert comes marching out and says that Catherine was a fine girl and you had seduced her. I said OK she's a fine girl but she's been around and you couldn't do it by yourself. Rosealee told Robert to go upstairs but he says no I'm Catherine's friend and I'm sticking up for her. I said Robert you are an ignorant little piss-ant who doesn't know anything about women. Then Orin's mother went in and stared at you like she wanted to cut off your head."

"That's terrible," Joseph interrupted. "I'm sorry you had to walk in on it."

"Sure it was awful but I didn't know and I wanted to go fishing." The doctor began wheezing and cackling at the same time. "Then I got angry and said it was between Rosealee and you, and you were groaning in your sleep as if you could hear all of this horseshit going on. I said big goddamn deal so Catherine was pretty and lonely and from an unhappy family so you made love. Why couldn't people make love without all this viciousness. Then I hugged Rosealee and she began crying and then stopped and you woke up."

Joseph put his face in his hands and let his head buzz around this information like a fly between window and screen. "I was a little drunk but I was going to tell Rosealee I was sorry."

"Sort of makes you want to cut off your pecker, doesn't it?" He laughed and poured another drink. "But you can't say you're sorry because you're not and Rosealee knows that in her heart. She probably knows when you take the kids to Chicago you will go into a hotel room and fuck like rabbits or minks so why would she believe you're sorry? You don't know

Jim Harrison: Farmer

———

95

anything about women. They're real smart about these things."

"So then what do I do? I started maybe with Catherine because I hadn't known many women other than Rosealee."

"Oh bullshit. People don't get love in their heart for a reason. They are open to it or not and when they're open it happens to them. With Rosealee you were open like a target since you were young. And you probably never forgave her for choosing Orin over you which any girl would, not because of your leg but because Orin was flashy and handsome. But also as worthless and unreliable as you are."

"I don't get what you mean." Joseph was startled; he had thought himself a sort of model of reliability and steadfastness. He was also embarrassed because the doctor had struck close about his treatment of Rosealee.

"Here's what I mean and right on the money." The doctor lit his pipe and stared at the steamy window. "I mean you sit in that farmhouse with your mother ten years since Carl died and in the middle of which Orin died and Rosealee was presented to you. What do you do with this fine woman? Nothing. You just hold back thinking more or less how life has screwed you to the wall. You agreed in your mind like your mother not to get over Carl. At least Carl laughed a lot and lived and worked hard though he was sort of a stupid shit about farming. Also his daughters. Until you came and after your brother died of diphtheria it was like the daughters didn't exist. With each one he was disappointed and your mother was heartbroken because she couldn't come up with the son he wanted. How do you think the girls felt? Sure he was nice to them but always, even after you came, they knew they weren't boys and knew they somehow failed their daddy who worked so hard and was still poor. It happens all over here. He wasn't the only farmer who marked his daughters as worthless. So when you came and Arlice came at the same time I said Carl you got another daughter and he said shit. Then I said you also got a son in the same batch and I had to be happy for him though at the same time I was angry. He started working hard then anyway. When your brother and also that sister died of disease the grief made him lazy. Grief makes people lazy because they can't understand why they should go on if they're going to die but they should go on harder if they understood it. Your mother died in a great way. She had more guts than you and Carl and me and ten more like us. So when the accident happened to you he blamed himself and became softer then. It was always heartbreaking to us all when he would carry you into the tavern on Saturday and you would be happy and he'd just sit there watching you drag your cast around the room talking to everyone like nothing had happened."

"Please stop!" Joseph's eyes welled with tears of exhaustion and the pain of what the doctor said.

"Fuck you. Why should I stop? So you can get off the hook? I'm an expert because my wife never even loved me, though other than that we had a good marriage even though one of us, I don't know which, couldn't make children. My sister's children were in Wales so it was grand to come visit because I liked your father and to see all you fine tow-headed children handsome and smart in that old run-down farmhouse. And the girls so bright I said to Carl these girls somehow have to go to college, let me help, and he just said no you help too much, they'd be better off married right away. It's pure and simple that old country bullshit. The Swedes are as formal and fucked-up as Japs, don't you know?"

Joseph slumped deeply in the seat. Three poplar leaves torn off in the storm were pasted against the windshield; then the one whose edge was curled peeled and blew away leaving its imprint for a moment before the rain washed it away. The rain became intermittent; its sound on the roof had made the doctor talk louder. The wind swept water from the leaves down in fresh showers but it was apparent that the main part of the storm had passed and with the passing Joseph's pulse

Jim Harrison: Farmer

97

slowed, his intense nervousness lessened into simple despair. He kept thinking of returning to some pre-disaster state but his mind held out the image of the safe place of his youth. Back in a corner of the mow in the barn he had made a rude house with boards down in the hay. Then he covered this sunken house leaving only its entry clear. When he was unhappy he would hide there with his pile of rabbit and raccoon skins, two sets of deer antlers, the dried head of a large pike he had tacked to a board, and his favorite blanket from his early childhood. When his pain after the accident made his eyes water he would scramble up the ladder above the cows and hide there for a few hours and the pain always seemed to subside. Even Orin didn't know his place though he once had allowed Arlice to come with him but then later when his parents had been worried she was prevailed upon to tell his secret so he had to move to another corner of the mow. When an uncle had given them the cattle blanket to use while kneeling on the ice when ice fishing Joseph had recognized it as truly belonging in his hideout.

The silence became uncomfortable and the doctor rolled down the window. Joseph opened his own and looked at the dark gray clouds still scudding along barely above treetops. The temperature had dropped abruptly and he shivered.

"You know, Yoey, I always thought it was odd you couldn't better apply what you learn from all you read to your own life. But then I just now thought though I'm a doctor and know so much about the body I smoke all the time and drink like crazy. I eat stuff that drives my stomach in circles and gives me the shits. I learned from your dad that herring is good with onions and bacon and eggs and potatoes for breakfast. So I eat it on Sunday mornings and sure enough it's dinner before my stomach is calm enough to take a drink. Of course I'm seventy-three but I've been acting this way since thirty. So it's no wonder you don't know anything either. So we're both ignorant bastards but if you're going to be ignorant you should at least make your mistakes on the side of life. Maybe what

Jim Harrison: Farmer

you've done with Catherine I mean isn't bad. Maybe it's good for both of you. But what's bad is what you haven't done with Rosealee. What you left out."

"Maybe I'm having a nervous breakdown," Joseph said haltingly. One of the sisters had sent his mother a subscription to the *Reader's Digest* for her birthday. Joseph barely ever peeked at it but late one sleepless night he had read an article about nervous breakdowns, then dreamed unhappily of pig brains when they butchered. How can brains do anything looking so gray and wet and unlike anything else on earth?

"Oh bullshit. Maybe so, but what does it mean? Often it means people are forced out of ruts by seeing certain facts of life they can't take into their systems. They're overloaded. So I give some tranquilizers which they take to make these facts less painful." The doctor got out of the car and leaned back into it to finish. "So if you got yourself a nervous breakdown it's about goddamn time. I probably shouldn't say this but right after the war Rosealee about cracked up because she discovered a letter this Italian woman sent Orin. So I told her he was away three years in battle did you want him to remain comfortless? I said to her I bet you get sexed up yourself and she started blushing and giggling. If I hadn't been a professional man I'd have had a go at it right there." The doctor laughed. "Let's look at the river."

The path down the bank to their favorite stretch of river had been gouged by the rain and the clay was slippery. The doctor carefully made his way grabbing at bushes to avoid slipping but Joseph fell and nearly knocked the doctor off his feet.

"You get your head that far up your ass and you can't even walk." Then he laughed as Joseph tried to wipe the clay from an elbow. "You look like you shit your pants." Joseph had slid on his seat in the clay.

The river was high and turbulent, clearly unwadable. They looked at it dolefully and lit cigarettes.

Jim Harrison: Farmer

———

99

"So what should I do? I know I got to stop the nonsense with Catherine or I think I do. But maybe I fooled Rosealee too long and she won't take me back."

"That just shows how dumb you are again. Of course she'll take you back but you got to let her breathe. You hit her over the head with a club and you just can't pick her off the ground and say I'm sorry ma'am, I didn't mean anything. Give her a few weeks or a month. And not until you quit fooling with that girl. If Rosealee was fooling with someone you'd be loading your gun or beating her up, neither of which she can do to you. And besides I'm sick of talking about it because if you can't figure it out by now it's a lost cause anyway."

They stopped at a bar and restaurant in Tustin and the doctor true to his form ate a T-bone and a pile of raw onion. Joseph only poked at his food because of the Dexedrine so the doctor speared his steak and finished it. Joseph felt dazed but somehow bursting with talk that he couldn't give voice to.

"I'm going to pay for this but it tastes good." The doctor wiped his chin and belched. "For years I've expected to die of a heart attack but as you can see it hasn't happened. I'll no doubt rot on the hoof like an old cow. I had some good fishing this month, then I had to tell these parents their little daughter had leukemia, and you know I couldn't fish then worth a shit, though in all these years I've told hundreds they were going to die. Children are different. They die like beautiful dogs who don't know what's happening to them except it hurts. Over in the Ardennes there was this boy in the grass who looked like he was sleeping. Our messenger. I said wake up wake up we got to get out of here but then I couldn't see in this wheat field that his leg was blown off and he was dead. And just an hour before we had found some wine in this French farmhouse and drunk it. It was good wine. But even that was easier than those parents and the child because she wouldn't live until eighteen like my friend the messenger. She will die at seven and when her parents die in who knows how many years their hearts will

Jim Harrison: Farmer

100

still be busted by it. This isn't good after-dinner kind of talk but I was thinking when I came out to the farm and you lay there on the table all bloody I could see right away at least you weren't going to die."

Joseph had a disturbing vision of himself lying on the table with his leg wet and twisted askew. So many times in the years later he had wanted to say *it doesn't matter it doesn't matter I'm still just me* when his parents were being overweaning. At least Arlice never mentioned it, they just continued playing and doing chores like always. Once when Charlotte had looked at him and burst into tears he had comforted her and said I feel fine. Joseph thought, we really can endure anything short of dying. Even Mother who kept reading and talking to her friends and ordered seed for the garden and made herself a summer dress on the sewing machine, though she knew summer was totally out of the question because she would be in a grave.

"You're a lot of fun to fish with." The doctor waved his hand in front of Joseph's face and Joseph ducked as if attacked. "My god I'm sorry. Let's go back and fish in the lake. We can put on poppers and catch some bass. That is if you aren't tired of this. I'd like to think it was doing me good but I'm fucked-up enough so I can't tell. Arlice once said after Rosealee chose Orin, I'm sorry Joseph but when you're upset you've got to talk. That pill makes me feel like I am going to jump out of my tired skin. What you said before about Dad and my sisters upset me but it was true. But he couldn't get to Arlice. She charmed him silly and I suppose it was because we were so close to each other and she was so pretty. Even I her brother knew she was that pretty. I was sad when she married. I couldn't bear to look at the man and when she divorced and married again I hated that man too even if he was better than the first." Joseph laughed realizing he was talking too loud. He remembered his anger when he found Arlice parked in a car with her worthless boyfriend. Her blouse was off and Joseph

Jim Harrison: Farmer

had pulled her boyfriend through the open car window. And Arlice had kept yelling it's OK it's OK.

"You probably get Arlice confused with Rosealee. Sometimes when you talk it uncaps the well so it won't blow up. You know these psychiatrists are probably worth it because they are someone to whom the troubled person can say anything. Once after we had been married for years my wife said at breakfast, I'm so sorry we can't have children, and we both broke down on the spot partly out of relief that we were admitting what we had been thinking about so long."

They paid the check and left. Joseph was deep enough in thought to stumble on the steps. "I used to think it would be fine to have children but then I thought I probably wouldn't make much of a father if they turned out to be girls. Just like my dad, do you think?"

At the lake they could see that the storm had passed through by the water in the rowboat which they bailed out with a rusty coffee can. They took turns rowing while the other fished. The lake was flat calm and they caught small bass and bluegills along the edge of the lily pads that skirted the shore. They saw a blue heron and a family of common loons with a half dozen young birds following the parents keeping well ahead of their rowboat. They were both mildly drunk but placid. Joseph felt sleepy and relaxed with his brain clear enough to work a way out of the mess.

"Tough shit. The big ones don't taste good," Joseph said. The doctor had lost a large bass when his line had wrapped around a log.

"Don't care. Bass are like beer you know, I don't want them unless there's nothing else around."

A water snake swam past the boat; the doctor poked at it with the tip of his flyrod and the startled snake turned and hissed. Then it continued on its way, leaving an S-shaped miniature wake in the water.

Jim Harrison: Farmer
———

"Is there a pill that would allow me to keep up with Catherine?"

"Not likely. It would be a bad pill to have within reach. If our bodies could keep up with our appetites we'd be a mess, don't you think? There are all these young men wanting to meet a nymphomaniac but they would properly get over that in a few hours. After a certain amount of affection everyone wants to lay back and think it over. Even the Queen of Sheba I expect. If you get into the wilderness and there's too many trout it's no fun after a little while."

Jim Harrison: Farmer

On Memorial Day morning Joseph walked out to the granary to check the harness he had packed in oil back in January. He remembered wiping the oil off his hands before he reached for Catherine in her absurdly diaphanous blue underthings. Part of the harness had come back with the oil treatment and appeared salvageable. His mind kept turning to the fact that after lunch he would have to pick some daisies and lilacs and visit the graves. It would be a hurried visit because he didn't want to talk to the people who generally spent the afternoon of Memorial Day walking around in hushed silence reminiscing in whispers about the lives of the dead. After he had cleaned the excess oil from the harness he lathered it with saddle soap, wiped away the foam, and hung the harness from spikes. The collars had proved too moldy to recover. He had sold Tom and Butch for a thousand dollars the month after his father died; many thought Joseph had been cheated but in grief he had wanted the horses off the farm. When the truck came and he loaded the team for the buyer he was unable to talk. The man noticed his discomfort and walked over to the fence pretending to look at the corn. Joseph spent a few moments pressing his face to each neck then moved quickly off the truck and walked to the house.

What grand plans they had organized for the team after winning so easily at the local fair for two years. They marked the calendar with a dozen fairs throughout the late summer and

Jim Harrison: Farmer

were sure the prize money however meager would cover their expenses. Einar would loan them his cattle truck to haul the horses. Einar and Joseph held the ends of the eveners while Carl held the reins. They would swing around to the load in front of the full grandstand and Carl would quickly climb up and mount the seat on the stoneboat and when Joseph and Einar would drop the eveners so the hitch would catch, Carl would shout. But the horses were keyed to the clink of the hitch. Their great flanks would drop and they surged forward tearing clods of hard-packed earth from the track. When they finished the pull the grandstand would cheer wildly. The audience was silent until the pull was finished because the horses would stop if they heard premature applause. Tom weighed twenty-four hundred and Butch about twenty-two—they had fed Butch up that last winter but hadn't got a chance to weigh him. Carl had made extra money skidding logs that last winter but only because he wanted to keep the team in shape. Joseph thought it was a joy to see him have a sport other than fishing and hunting after so many years of hard work. Carl always treated fishing and hunting as basically food gathering which disgusted the doctor because Carl rarely admitted how much fun he was having. Einar wanted to buy the team when Carl died but Joseph said no he didn't want to see them in the county with their deep chestnut color and flaxen manes and fetlocks. The harness was thrown into an empty bin in the granary and remained there for a decade.

Joseph looked up when he heard a car. It was Cathcrine's Jeep and his stomach churned. Oh god. Chicago was three days away and that had to be the end of it. But the major got out of the Jeep and Joseph remembered the doctor's warning. Holy christ I'm going to be shot. Or maybe he wants to go fishing I hope. Joseph walked out on the steps of the granary and waved. The major walked toward him; even in his late fifties he looked trim and official.

"Fine Memorial Day. I was sorry to hear about your mother. But Catherine said she had cancer. Can I come in?"

Jim Harrison: Farmer

———

105

"Yes. Sure." Joseph led the way back up the steps into the granary. "Watch where you sit, I've been oiling some harness."

"I bought that in Atlanta." The major saw the jug on the windowsill.

"Jesus I forgot." Joseph hefted the jug. It was minus the half he had drunk that New Year's Day with Catherine. She had spit out her taste claiming she liked only wine. He handed it to the major. "Sorry I don't have a cup."

The major drank deeply, looked around the granary and drank again. "I was going to start by talking about fishing." He handed Joseph the jug and Joseph's hand shook. "I see your hand is shaking. I know why. I know everything because I heard Robert and Catherine talking downstairs. You're not going to marry Catherine?"

"I guess not." It came out almost as a whisper. "It would be dumb. I'm not her sort."

"What is her sort?" The major raised his eyebrows. He fiddled with his hat which had fishing flies in the sheepskin band.

"Well someone rich and educated, you know?" Joseph paused. For some reason his nervousness was dissipating. "Someone who is sophisticated and lives in a city and is closer to her age."

"I wanted you to know I wasn't fooled and I don't like to be fooled." The major drank again. "I moved up here partly to get away but Catherine has had a good year. Maybe her best year yet. You must be in your forties and I don't know how you lead your life but I'd have to guess you aren't experienced in these things." He paused and stared at Joseph who met his gaze directly.

"No. I guess I'm not. It was the first time for me to do such a thing. I couldn't seem to help myself, even when I knew it was wrong." Joseph drank then coughed. He was sure the major didn't have a gun but was past caring.

"I think you were wrong too. But I can't blame you be-

Jim Harrison: Farmer

106

cause knowing Catherine I know it was probably less than half your idea. I can't say what's going on in her mind. You're decent, I know that. She's flighty like her mother and gets bored easily. If she were a normal young girl I might shoot you. Only she's not and I'm not fool enough to be blind to that. But I don't like to be fooled. There's nothing to do though." Now the major was nervous and leaned forward. "Should you apologize or what?"

"I'm sorry. I can't say I wish I'd never met your daughter." Joseph stood and looked out the window. "I'd never met a girl like her but I'm still sorry." Joseph turned and the major stood. "I can imagine how you feel though I never had a daughter."

"As a matter of fact I don't feel anything. It's happened before. I just thought you shouldn't try to marry her. You are more misused yourself than someone who took advantage, I'm not that much of a fool. I always thought a son would be easier to raise but I'm not sure. Anyway I know she wouldn't be happy for long if she married you."

"She talked of it and I didn't say anything. She'll get over it easy enough I think." They stepped out on the porch. The geese came around the corner of the pigpen and began honking. Joseph was clearly relieved.

"Maybe we can fish some evening?" The major offered his hand and they shook. "I simply wanted to get this cleared up. You probably thought about what might happen if I found out. It was a bad thing to do and our lives are filled with bad things. Only, as a father I have to think who it might have been if you hadn't been the one. Do you know what I mean?"

Joseph nodded. They walked toward the house but then the major asked if he could look at Catherine's horse. They walked into the barn and the major began talking about beef prices. He was raising some Hereford steers and wanted Joseph's opinion on what auction to buy some more at, or whether Joseph thought a cow-calf operation was a better idea. Joseph said he thought the major would be better off in a small

Jim Harrison: Farmer

---

cow-calf operation. He could always borrow a bull for a few weeks and besides it was more interesting. Joseph retrieved the jug from the granary and then went into the house and made sandwiches. The major finally left at midafternoon. He reminded Joseph sadly of Orin; the major had become a career man out of excitement and after two wars he was burned out and had no interest in more ordinary activities. Cattle and fishing were enough, a wife and daughter far too complicated and confusing.

Before the major left he helped Joseph pick two large bouquets of lilacs. Joseph thought that odd but when the major suggested they spend the rest of the afternoon fishing he said that he had to take flowers to the cemetery.

"I was an orphan," the major said, carefully selecting a branch to cut with his jackknife. "But I made it to the Point and I moved up fast because of the war. Rosealee's husband was a pilot, wasn't he?"

"Yes. He went down in the China Sea they told us. That's who these other flowers are for." Joseph paused and brushed away a bee. "He was my best friend." The statement was so stark and matter of fact that Joseph could nearly see Orin beside him. The thickness of the lilacs made a good hiding place when they played cowboys.

"You people are lucky to be so close and honor the dead this way." The major waved at the farm. "When I came up here fishing years ago I knew I was going to hide out and fish and die here."

"I guess we're a lot luckier than the dead or the evidence says so." Joseph laughed at the thought. "Sometimes I wonder, don't you? You probably saw enough that this place looks real good. I think it's a fine place, though I don't know any other."

The major handed Joseph the flowers. "Catherine said you were going to the ocean this summer but when I asked her which ocean she didn't know. She's so scatterbrained I don't think she belongs in this world."

Jim Harrison: Farmer

"Maybe I'm addled too because I'm not sure which myself. I made a list of the advantages of each. But probably the Pacific up in Oregon because Florida is too hot."

They turned as the doctor drove into the yard. He read their faces from the car and got out affably. "I just pulled some tonsils and I'm going fishing. Hello, Major." He smiled at Joseph and looked at their bouquets. "Going up to the cemetery? You better wait. I saw Rosealee there when I drove past. How's the wife?" he asked the major.

"Awful as usual. I found her in town yesterday." The major smiled. "I make her drive the Jeep so if she hits anything she's less likely to get hurt."

"We'll send her away for a dry-out. I'm not interrupting anything am I?"

Joseph and the major said no in frantic unison and the doctor laughed. "Well I'm glad you didn't shoot him," he said to the major. "He's a good boy."

They all laughed, the major and Joseph nervously. The major went off fishing with the doctor leaving the Jeep in the yard. Joseph stood dumbly with his two bouquets thinking that if Rosealee saw the Jeep she would think Catherine was there. But then he partly wished Catherine were there so he could forget about the cemetery, forget about everything on earth in fact. He put the lilacs in the car and went into the house to wash and dress for Memorial Day.

There were a half-dozen cars at the small country cemetery. The grounds were kept up by the Swedish Lutheran church but others were buried there too. The Lutheran minister had gladly accepted a Catholic suicide who was refused consecrated ground. The minister considered Catholics to be barbarians in this respect, worse than the Baptists who were so worried about avoiding dancing, drinking, movies, and fornication that they forgot the Lord. The minister always spent Memorial Day afternoon at the cemetery to comfort the bereaved, though he inevitably ended up talking about the

Jim Harrison: Farmer

weather or the prospects this year for the Detroit Tigers. He saw Joseph pull up and greeted him rather unctuously.

"A fine day Joseph."

"Yup." Joseph stood there with the two bouquets feeling silly. He had no more to say. He wanted to place the flowers and go home. "See you again some day," he nodded to the preacher, feeling foolish. He had always driven his mother to church, at least until she was too sick, but he would sit out in the car through the service reading the Sunday paper with resolute thoroughness. The preacher no doubt knew every move he made but Joseph gave less than a shit. Orin's mother was Methodist and Rosealee was nothing but she had endured countless Sundays of nonsense without complaint. Joseph walked toward their plot through an aisle of blooming yellow forsythia and small flowering crab trees. It was hot and he carried his coat. About fifty yards away he could see Rosealee, Orin's mother, and Robert on a blanket. Robert was reading a book.

Joseph laid the one bouquet between his father's stone and his mother's fresh grave. Her death date had not been added yet but his read CARL JOSEPH LUNDGREN 1882-1946. The stone was a simple slab, unadorned. Arlice wanted a big stone but his mother insisted that that would be immodest. The two children were there with small granite plaques, CARL JR and DORTHEA both dead in 1909, he at four and she at three years, of diphtheria. Joseph lifted the flowers and put them between their two stones. Four and three. What grief on earth. There were small cherubs carved in the corners of the stones. How could anyone bear it and not go mad he thought. CARL JR whom his father never spoke of and DORTHEA also never mentioned. He did not have the guts for it, pure and simple. His eyes watered not for his parents but for the children, and the odor of the forsythia began to sicken him. They died his mother said within a week of one another, Dorthea first, then Carl Jr. It was their first year on the farm and she said no one would think that children could get sick in such a beautiful

Jim Harrison: Farmer

place. She said his father had broken the front window with his head when Carl Jr. died.

Joseph walked over to where Orin was buried with his father beside him. Orin's mother got up to greet him as if his gesture outweighed everything he could have done to Rosealee.

"Hello, Yoey. God bless you." She took the flowers from him and propped them against Orin's headstone. They hugged as they did once a year before Orin's grave, as if it were the only thing they shared. Rosealee got up then, though Robert continued reading with a petulant look.

"Hello, Joseph. It's a beautiful day. The doctor was here." Rosealee looked worn, nearly haggard.

"When you're willing to talk let me know." He averted his eyes from her gaze.

"Maybe we can talk when you get back from Chicago." She turned and went back to the blanket.

At home Joseph sat at the table until twilight. On the top of the chest of drawers at the far end of the room there were pictures of all seven of them by order of birth with Carl Jr. first and Joseph last. Dorthea most closely resembled Arlice but with even more delicate lines while Carl Jr. was thin and lacked Joseph's broad features. The pictures were all taken on or around their third birthdays. The photographer, Lindquist, was a distant cousin and was so taciturn he barely made a living. The photos were somber, without a smile among the seven. Joseph remembered with delight one of Roselee's kindergartners, who looked a little like Carl Jr. The child was the bastard son of the daughter of the grain operator. The daughter had gone off to college in Chicago after the war and had returned with the son. His name was Samuel and he was a *Wunderkind*. There was talk that his father was a Jew and a college professor. Samuel was the smallest child in school and also the brightest Rosealee had ever taught. He could read well at five and used to gather the others around him and read them stories

Jim Harrison: Farmer

---

when Rosealee was busy. One day almost to her alarm he read a long story from an empty notebook making it up as he went along. All of the students were addicted to him and the older boys taught him an obscene song that he sang happily in his pure, thin voice to amuse them. One afternoon he astounded them all by learning his multiplication tables during the half-hour recess after being bribed with a dime to see if he could do it. Rosealee told the superintendent and he sent a man out to test Samuel and the somewhat pompous man discovered that Samuel's IQ was 180, or as high as the test measured. There was a small piece in the newspaper about it but Samuel remained nonchalant. Joseph thought his most endearing talent was not his brain but his propensity for dancing without music. At recess or even when he was walking dreamily around the schoolroom he would regularly break into an involved jig as if listening to some music in his head that no one else could hear. He would make two or three little pointed goat steps then whirl around prancing, blind to his surroundings. Often the other children would clap and cheer, though the performance wasn't for them. Joseph once saw him dancing along the road on the way to school, utterly alone. They were depressed when Samuel didn't show up for school the following year.

Joseph had often wondered if Keats and Walt Whitman were like Samuel when they were young. He got up from the table and found his Modern Library Keats but it was getting too dark to read and he didn't feel up to having a light on. It saddened him that he had never managed to get his students very interested in Keats or Whitman, or biology or mathematics for that matter. But he knew that he himself had learned by rote and his true interest in these matters had only arrived in his early twenties. Up until then he had thought as his students did that knowledge was a faraway land and not a very interesting one at that, and the description of the land had to be learned as a rite of passage, a necessary though temporary interference in their way from childhood through puberty to adulthood. But to the truly gifted one like Samuel or John Keats, knowledge was

Jim Harrison: Farmer

as real as a leaf or a mud puddle. They found music to dance to in the most ordinary things. They did not live with distant thoughts of the ocean, or endure countless monotonous days in order to hunt or fish or simply read about hunting and fishing and the Indian and Caribbean and Arctic oceans. Joseph believed that Keats and Whitman and young Samuel somehow lived in the purest reaches of their imaginations and there was a beauty in it that wasn't found in the preoccupations of others; say making a living which turned out to be nothing other than what comes simply and directly to most animals.

Once a few years back Joseph had been forced to take two summer courses to keep his certificate. He had been mournful about his six weeks in Ann Arbor, a town he loathed on sight with its smelly, polluted Huron River. But a teacher, an old man with long white hair, had made them read a dozen books in six weeks and Joseph's mind fairly reeled, even though he spent much of the time dreaming about the trout fishing he was missing. It was a course in short novels and stories and they read Dostoevski's *Notes from Underground*, Gogol's *The Overcoat*, Tolstoi's "The Cossacks," James Joyce's "The Dead," Melville's *Billy Budd*, Faulkner's "The Bear," and works of Katherine Anne Porter and Glenway Wescott and Sherwood Anderson.

Joseph had liked "The Bear" the best but was troubled deeply by the Dostoevski book. How could a man feel that way and not blow his brains out? The professor had chided Joseph by saying that it was not Dostoevski but the character he created who was talking. He liked Sherwood Anderson least because he wrote only about what everyone knows, but the professor insisted that that was precisely why he was good, a point of view that flew over Joseph's head like a migrating teal. The professor frequently called on Joseph to speak but it seemed to Joseph that he was only being used to illustrate the wrong point of view and he grew adamant and silent.

The pain of his weeks in Ann Arbor was alleviated only by Rosealee's three-day visit. They went to the symphony for the

Jim Harrison: Farmer

first time and were shocked by the power of the experience which was so unlike listening to the radio. Rosealee said it was as if the music entered your skin, not just your ears, and after that Joseph often listened to classical music late at night on the radio when he had trouble sleeping. One evening they were walking down University Place and saw the professor staring in a bookstore window. They exchanged small talk and went into a bar. Joseph's notions that the professor was a boozer were confirmed and he was irked by the way the man charmed Rosealee by his learned talk. But the conversation turned to birds, which were the professor's avocation, and the following summer he stopped by to see the nesting osprey that Joseph had told him about. They had all had dinner together at this very table. The professor had brought wine in his car trunk but noticing Joseph's distaste had gone back to the car for a bottle of scotch which Joseph thought tasted like Ivory soap. Rosealee was gay, effervescent, but Joseph's mother had been shy at having so educated a man in the house. She relaxed only late in the evening when the professor began singing music hall songs from the twenties in a baritone that was full despite an occasional quavering note.

Now he turned on the radio but couldn't find any classical music. He recognized only a few pieces. It was totally dark and he began to think about supper but there was nothing much in the refrigerator so he fried some eggs and ate them with some cold beef and horse-radish. Perhaps the doctor and the major might drop in after fishing. What if Catherine stopped by while her father was here? But she would see the Jeep in the yard. Every evening they had sat here to listen to the war news—the girls had all left home by then—and Gabriel Heatter could make a minor triumph comforting as Hitler swept across Europe. Joseph had pinned a map of Europe to the wall so they could trace what they knew of Orin's movements. After the war Orin took him up in a rented Stinson Voyager and quite literally scared the piss out of him by stalling the plane on purpose. He had been angry at the trick for days. Orin lived on

Jim Harrison: Farmer

114

adrenaline and had gotten himself into some nasty fights at the tavern out of boredom. He was happy when the Korean War arrived though it certainly lacked the grandness of the other one.

Joseph took a cup of coffee out to the porch swing and sat there listening to the creaking of its rusty hinges and to the frogs from the swamp that were so relentless that people forgot the noise existed. What a wonderful map of Europe with his own trip planned for 1949 traced across England *but then I didn't go because Chevrolet had that Powerglide without a clutch and it was pleasant not to have to thump unsurely at a clutch with my leg. And another one last year when the first became so battered and unstable that Rosealee didn't want to ride in it. I have to get off my dead ass and get her to forgive me or I'm sunk. My mind is going or maybe like the doctor said it is just opening up. He came out when Dad had the flu and I hitched up the horses to see if I could somehow sneak off and do some plowing but I never even got the plow attached. A stray dog came by and the mare hated dogs and I was dragged like a goddamn fool around the barnyard by the team yelling whoa whoa whoa and finally dragged on my stomach until Mother came out and got hold of their halters. Then the doctor had to clean off my stomach and chest which was a mess but Mother looked funny leading the horses back to the barn. I was embarrassed and after he wrapped me up I went out and took the harness off. Dad was angry but I said I at least had to give it a try. And only a week later Arlice and Rosealee were standing around in back of the barn and Orin said I bet you a dollar I can ride that goddamn cow so I naturally said I bet you a dollar I can ride it. We both got thrown badly and Orin was knocked out. The cow never trusted me after that and Dad could never figure out why she was nervous when he milked her and I was around. Rosealee and Arlice thought Orin was dead but I said he's just knocked out like in boxing. Orin caught the greased pig at the fair by getting wet and rolling in sand and gravel so it stuck to him. He was the only one who*

Jim Harrison: Farmer

could get any purchase on the animal but he was disqualified
for cheating.

The doctor's car pulled in with bugs already crowding around the headlights. They jumped from the car and for a moment Joseph thought something might be wrong.

"You missed it tonight, buddy. I saved two for your breakfast but look what Major got." The major held up a fish but Joseph couldn't see it well. They went into the kitchen and put the fish in the sink. It was a male brown trout with a heavy lower jaw and deep brown and gold colors. The major looked pale and his eyes were glazed with excitement.

"That's a rare fish, my friend," Joseph said. He was clearly jealous never having caught a brown that big on fly.

"I got it just before dark above that log jam. There were so many mayflies I caught fish after fish but when I tightened up on this one I knew I had something." The major did a little dance around the kitchen and Joseph suddenly was quite happy for him.

"He was screaming like a pig and I thought he was drowning." The doctor's face was glowing. "Let's see what he was feeding on." The doctor deftly opened the stomach with his jackknife.

Jim Harrison: Farmer
———

D espite her anger over Joseph's unfaithfulness Rosealee had managed to persuade the seniors to put off their trip to Chicago for a week. They sniped a bit but Daniel sagely remarked that "it's not every day your mother dies." He had done well on the final exams Rosealee had administered for Joseph in his short but necessary mourning period. Rosealee trusted them on what she called an "honor system" and, besides, she had her own young charges in the other room to attend to. Daniel was very keyed up about the Chicago trip. Now that it was delayed they would get to see the White Sox and the Tigers play instead of the White Sox and the Yankees. They were all terribly excited, none of them having been to Chicago before except Catherine whose nasty blasé attitude irritated everyone except Daniel, who was far beyond noticing such things. All the boys liked to stand around when Catherine shot baskets or played softball in a skirt for any glimpse of a promised land that had been denied to all of them except, they believed, Robert who was always with her. Only the other girls understood Catherine's purposeful wantonness, the way she flung herself around for the boys; she was so obvious she even got on the children's swings one afternoon and laughed as her audience of young bucks gathered for the show trying very hard to be nonchalant.

Joseph had just got to bed after an exhausting full day's fishing trip with the doctor when the phone rang. He hoped it

Jim Harrison: Farmer

was Rosealee not Catherine—in his extreme state he couldn't bear the thought of Catherine, especially after the way the doctor had dredged up the past. And he dreaded her plans for Chicago when they at last would be able to make love in a bed.

"Joe?" The voice barely whispered.

"Yes. Who is it for Christ's sake?" The whisper startled him.

"It's me, Ted. You know. At the bar. Look I got to talk quiet. Your brother-in-law from Flint is here with these two other guys. He thinks you took the seniors to Chicago and I heard him talking about your Dad's coins. I think he's going to swipe them. They just got another drink but I'd get ready if I was you."

"Thanks, Ted. I will."

"Just thought I'd warn you. The guy's an asshole."

"I know, Ted. Thanks. Bye now."

How comic Joseph thought. Mother a few weeks dead and buried and that fuckhead up here to scavenge, thinking I'm in Chicago. Frank had always wanted those coins. Joseph stood in his underpants scratching his head. Two guys with him. It was like a cowboy movie. Since the first year of World War II when their fortunes had modestly improved his father had tossed coins into a pickle crock in the corner of the dining room; after his father died Joseph continued the custom. There were even some old Swedish coins a cousin had pitched in. Frank saved coins and had a book that stated their worth. Whenever he and Charlotte came north to the farm Frank would eye the coins and sort through the top layer. Joseph had always teased him that the old ones were at the bottom and if the "rainy day" ever came when he needed the money he might let Frank have a peek. Joseph assigned a nephew at family gatherings to keep watch on Frank and the coins and there had been an embarrassing scene when he had been caught pocketing several of them.

Joseph stood there wondering what to do, then walked to a

Jim Harrison: Farmer

closet and drew his deer rifle from the case. It was an old slide action .35 Remington with a variable Bushnell scope. He found a half-dozen shells, turned out all the lights, and walked to the barn, still in his underpants. It was a warm still night with the air moist and dew on the grass. There was a three-quarter moon and when he got to the barn he studied the silvery roof of the house in the moonlight and the driveway sheltered by the maples. The driveway was also silver where it emerged from the maples and its hedge of lilac. The lilacs helped keep the snow off the driveway in the winter and now were just bursting into fragrant purple and white blossoms. His mother said that the lilacs were the first thing she had planted when they bought the farm.

Joseph went into the barn and climbed up into the mow. The steps were painful against his bare feet, especially on his bad leg. He walked across the old hay chaff and unlatched the mow door. He felt oddly distant and pleased that something so crudely *actual* was going to happen. The only thing he worried about was whether the rifle was properly sighted in but it had worked OK on the dogs. He took his underpants off and wiped the dust from the scope. Then he put them back on and hefted the rifle. He aimed at a tree, at the North Star, and at the Big Dipper. He aimed at the moon and noticed that you could see the unlit part of it through the rifle's scope. He adjusted the scope from 3x to 8x, bringing the moon five times closer to the barn. What a wonderful trick. He racked one shell into the chamber and four more into the breech. The brass was cool and he stuck the extra shell over his ear like a cigarette but it fell to the floor. He searched for the cartridge with his toes but couldn't find it. Five should be enough he thought while the mosquitoes began to find their target as he waited for his. I'm going to get my ass bit off. Then far off down the gravel road he saw the twin lights coming slowly. Then the lights went out as they drew nearer and Joseph laughed at the idea that Frank, like in the movies, had turned off his lights and was driving by

Jim Harrison: Farmer
———
119

moonlight. But when they pulled into the driveway the car lights came back on and Joseph assumed that they thought the house was for sure deserted. The men got out and he could hear their voices across the barnyard but couldn't make out what they were saying. Then Frank talked louder and he could see his short plump figure in the glare of headlights. Joseph sighted down on him and twisted the scope up until his head fairly filled the cross hairs. Frank was saying now rather loudly, you just wait here and if the crock's too heavy I'll call and then we'll get the fuck out of here pronto. Frank laughed. The other two leaned against the hood drinking from beer bottles. As Frank's laugh faded in the still night with the motor ticking and bugs already gathering around the lights, Joseph swung on the left headlight and pressed the trigger as the cross hairs centered it. There was blue flame and the hollow yet crisp explosion and the light went out, its shattering lost in the rifle shot which echoed through the outbuildings and dully against the house. There were screams and then a yell of holy christ as they scrambled to get into the car. Joseph lifted the rifle and racked and fired four more shots in the air. They backed swerving out of the driveway and down the road. Joseph watched them turn the corner a mile away; he was breathing heavily though very happy.

Back in the house he poured a nightcap and was surprised at how simple it all seemed compared to his other problems. It had been fun enough to partly make up for the abortive fishing earlier in the day. Were it not for Charlotte and the kids he knew he would have been quite happy blowing off Frank's head. But then he was disturbed at the idea of the mess and also the thought of chickens. At one moment they were scratching in the yard and the next moment you killed one for dinner by chopping off its head and the neck would spout blood. Oddly, Joseph could never remember looking back at the head itself immediately after the hatchet fell.

Joseph's sleep was so profoundly troubled that he spent a

Jim Harrison: Farmer

120

good deal of the night restlessly looking around the room with the bedlight on, trying to read. Twice he stared out a back window to make sure none of the outbuildings were on fire; fire had always been the ultimate rural horror, a burning barn could wipe out someone with any possible help far away and useless. First in his dreams there were the innards of the trout and the large gob of wet, partially digested mayflies. But they were cleaning the trout in Chicago and Catherine was hugging the major suggestively while a building burned in the background. Joseph tried to draw their attention to the fire but the doctor was separating the organs of the trout with a surgical knife. Then Joseph decided to sleep with the light on, but the light became the sun in a dream and he was making love in a field beside the ocean with a woman he assumed was Rosealee, but it turned out to be an older version of Catherine and much more lovely than she was now. Then when he slept again, Catherine regained her youth but was less slight, more whorish, and somehow infinitely more exciting, though Arlice was sitting in the room with them talking. Then Joseph was in the plane diving with Orin and that woke him for good barely after dawn.

He wondered how it was that dreams could carry a day, whether good or bad. If bad, it was as if a person woke up and their mind fairly ached, and the early morning reality of chores, breakfast, and driving to school lacked the energy to assert itself enough to dispel the dream. But the same was true if the dreams were particularly good, or if they were powerful sexual dreams which Joseph recognized most people had. You could dream about a homely girl and in class the next day she would be cast in a new, strange light though it tended to dissipate as the day grew. And dreams had the power to fool with reality, sometimes in a pathetic way; one dawn he had dressed in a hurry and rushed from the house dreaming that his father was out loading the crates of potatoes on the wagon. But halfway across the snowy barnyard he wondered why it was winter because it had been a warm autumn day in his dream. There

Jim Harrison: Farmer

was no wagon in the snowy fields and his father had been dead for three years.

Joseph threw grain to the chickens and geese wondering whom he might give them to. His dreams still held him and he stared vacantly around the barnyard hoping that Catherine would stop by. Why had he been rude to her when it was almost over anyway? Now he could feel the remnants of her dream appearance in the pit of his stomach but he could scarcely call her on the phone. Hello, Major, may I speak to your daughter? He stood smiling until he thought of Rosealee. Jesus. I can't make a mess of it after this many years. Of course I can, just continue the way I'm going now. Full circle in thirty years, only Orin is not here to take her, I'm pushing her away.

On impulse he walked to the barn and saddled Catherine's horse, riding straight back along the fence toward the state forest. The horse wagged its head at each fence post in mock alarm, then shied at an old plow leaning against a rock pile. Joseph wished that he had used a bit rather than a hackamore for better control. He laughed at how little the horse had been ridden and decided to give both himself and the horse a good workout. He cut across the corner of the pasture to the far gate, the horse knee-high in the timothy and the first purple heads of vetch that formed elongated buds and was sometimes thick enough to make a whole pasture purple. When he got down to open the gate the horse shied again when the gate creaked, pulling the reins from his hand. Oh jesus. The horse backed away as he approached exchanging step for step in a not very funny game. But Joseph used an old trick: he sat down with his back to the horse and whistled. Within a few moments the horse was nuzzling his shoulder and he remounted.

They entered the fringe of forest where there were hardwoods along a ridge. At one time they collected enough sap from the maples to make syrup for their own use and a little to give away. They used the same huge black pot in which they scalded the pigs when butchering and it took a half day of scrubbing to get the pig smell out of the metal. His father and neighbors sometimes drank too much while watching the sap boil but someone was always alert enough to catch it at the right moment. The kettle was hung from a large tripod made of pine poles.

On the far side of the ridge the conifers began, mixed with stands of poplar; the sandy soil supported not much more ground cover than brake, fern, and saplings except in the lower swampy areas. They entered a small grassy clearing which was thought of as an Indian graveyard by hearsay. It could have been Ottawa, Ojibwa, or Chippewa. Once he and Orin had decided to do some digging there but his mother, who was superstitious, forbade it. A friend of hers had gone repeatedly to an Indian known only as "Chief" who lived in a shack by the river in town. The Indian claimed to be a faith healer and many women reported relief from arthritis though the very idea disgusted Dr. Evans. He said their cures came from the amount of alcohol in the patent medicine they habitually swilled. But some of the women were Fundamentalist and weren't allowed the whiskey and aspirin treatment he advised for severe arthritic pain.

Joseph let the horse crop at the grass remembering that Whitman said grass was "the beautiful uncut hair of graves," a line that had always puzzled him. One day in class an otherwise simple pupil suggested that it might mean that the earth is so old someone is buried nearly everywhere. That might be it. But looking down over the horse's nose it was hard to imagine bones deep beneath the surface. Of course it was all unimaginable, and this had been the year that it became far more unimaginable than ever before. He looked up at the clouds and felt ill at ease in the still clearing. *I let so many years pass like smoke or just dreams though not even as real as the dreams of last night. But how can I do it differently if I'm not sure what I've done wrong? Of course not, dumbass, you don't get a mes-*

Jim Harrison: Farmer

123

sage like the skywriter at the fair telling you and everyone else what kind of beer to drink. The horse started at a snake wiggling through the grass, and Joseph soothed it by talking. "That's just a snake in an Indian graveyard." The horse wasn't reassured.

They continued on along the ridge above the creek then descended into the narrow valley at the end of which was the beaver pond and the beginning of the marsh. He lightly tethered the horse to a log and sat down after taking a drink of the cold water. At the far end of the pond a moulting duck scooted into the cattails to hide. On the far side of the pond along a clay bank there were slide marks where the beaver had dragged in fresh poplar to repair damage done in the spring runoff. This had always been Joseph's favorite place, even in his youth when it had provided the equivalent in the natural world of his fort in the hay mow. But now he was grasping hard for a peace that refused to arrive. He closed his eyes and got only the nude swimming bodies of Rosealee and Arlice for his pains. How hard they had all tried to be casual and adult about their nakedness. Like under the lamplight in Orin's living room when he went mad and demanded to see Rosealee in the light. But she thought finally that it had been wonderful and if it hadn't been for Catherine it *would* have been wonderful. Why hadn't he listened to Orin ten years before when Orin said night after night *Joseph you got to get out of here, you're not really going to farm and there's a whole world out there*. Then as the evening progressed his brain whirled with Orin's tales of far-off places and English, French, Italian, and Spanish women. And he said what if Rosealee knew what you've been up to while she sat here waiting, but Orin insisted it was different in wartime when you are away over three years and besides she knew something anyway. The day Orin had left for the Korean War Joseph and Rosealee took him to town for the train and Orin had drawn him aside with little Robert standing there white as a sheet and said you better get out of

Jim Harrison: Farmer

here before your life is over just spent in these goddamn sticks.

Joseph threw some pebbles into the pond remembering a time when he couldn't throw a stone all the way across and how pleased he had been when he finally reached the other side. Arlice had said too back in forty-six the first time at Dad's funeral, Joseph you should leave this place. My husband could get you a job on a newspaper or something. Are you just sitting around to see if Rosealee and Orin split up? Maybe he was. But he couldn't take the idea of Arlice's husband getting him a job. You're not staying here because of Mother? She doesn't need you, she has friends and can get along. Orin said that too. So why hadn't he left and why had he let so many years slip away like smoke? But that was easy. It was Rosealee mixed with Father and Mother, then Mother alone. Also taking the seniors to Detroit or Chicago in June and seeing those places as not so much squalid as places where he just wouldn't fit in. And the rituals of fishing and hunting. But even the doctor said Joseph why don't you see the world or at least your own country. The neighbor would feed the cattle. And the doctor had been angry when he backed out on England and bought a Powerglide instead. Goddamn your stupid foot which you use to get out of going places. The doctor said that when he was drunk, then apologized and never said it again.

The horse had lathered heavily by the time they reached the pond so he waited for the animal to cool before he let it have water. Now the horse drank deeply, lifting its head to stare at a waterbug swimming past its nose. Arlice had struck closest to home when she said if you're so interested in marine biology why don't you go to college and study it? You haven't even taken a look at the ocean. They used to worry so much about Arlice as if she were some sort of lost, incalculably precious jewel. She had gone to the teachers college in Mount Pleasant then run off with an actor to New York. The actor was in his thirties and had come to the college in a traveling Shakespeare play. What a scandal it had been and in the thirties they never

Jim Harrison: Farmer

———

125

saw her though she wrote she had become a Communist. Even that wasn't so terrible as her father was basically a Populist who read Herbert Croly and Lincoln Steffens and whose hero had been Eugene Debs. Then her actor-husband had disappeared in the Spanish Civil War without any of them having met him. She married again and this man was educated and had become rich after the war. Joseph met him only once and despised him on sight but then later decided he might be fine for Arlice. They had spent two days on the farm one summer and the man scarcely went outside. He was much older than Arlice and puffy looking but very sophisticated. He kept wanting to talk about economics and farm prices. Later he sent Joseph Samuelson's book on economics so that he wouldn't be "lost in history." But when they had sat around the table that evening arguing with Arlice and Mother sitting there too for a while, he had merely explained to the man that there *were* no economics in any elaborate sense involved in their farm life, which already with the press of events was quickly dwindling into the past. It was a subsistence or more exactly an "existence" on earth. A man came from Sweden, mostly to escape conscription as thousands did in the eighties and nineties. This particular man came from a family of fishermen near Örnsköldsvik but when he got there and worked in Chicago for three years he didn't like the city, so he took his young wife and two children, the first two of seven, and moved into northern Michigan because it was a beautiful place. They had seen it on an excursion train. They also had taken a train to Wyoming, but that seemed too wild, untamable and not all that long since the Indian wars had ceased. So they came up and bought a small farm for seven hundred dollars just after the century's turn, not to make money but to have a way to live. They had almost folded with the deaths of their first two children. Carl wasn't even a good farmer but he raised his children without any actual hunger or privation.

Swede immigrants were a trifle happy and dopey having

Jim Harrison: Farmer

126

escaped an essentially feudal situation, Arlice's husband had said. Maybe that's true Joseph said but there's not much in the way of economics to the whole thing. Sure we got cheated. If you hauled your crop to the railroad siding without first agreeing on a price you would be gypped. But we had the Grange and could hold out and there wasn't that much trouble until the Depression and then those who held extra-big mortgages and bought too much equipment or specialized in a single crop took a nose dive. The man said it must have been bleak. Joseph said it probably was bleak as hell but we didn't really have the advantage of knowing anything else. I'm not bleak now and neither is Arlice. But Arlice escaped it he said. Well my students continue later in life being pretty much the way they were in school. I bet it was bleaker in the cities. A lot of country people never owned a stock and when they tightened their belts they still had their land and animals and dancing, games, church, and parties.

When they left the man accepted with delight a dozen ducks and partridge to take back on the plane to New York. Once for Christmas Joseph had sent Arlice and her husband air freight a whole saddle of venison in dry ice with all of the empty spaces in the box filled with mallard, grouse, woodcock, and a few rabbits. Within a month Joseph received by parcel post a new set of the *Encyclopaedia Britannica*. He revered it in private for three years then took it down to the school where the children were advised that they must wash their hands before they used it.

Something disturbed his field of vision; at the far end of the pond where it seeped from the marsh a muskrat raised its head from the water and studied Joseph and the horse, then slowly submerged. Within a few seconds the muskrat appeared again peeking around the end of a log and wrinkling its nose, the better to pick up scent. The horse shook its head to rid itself of flies and the muskrat disappeared abruptly with a splash of its tail. They were a foolish, curious sort of mammal, but quickly

Jim Harrison: Farmer

127

replaced any severe predations by having another litter in the spring.

The marsh was saturated with life and, other than spring when there was a certain comfort in rediscovering that the earth was alive, he liked it best in early autumn when the birds went into a frenzy of regrouping in flocks to fly back south. There would be great clouds of blackbirds, starlings, and smaller groups of songbirds swooping about making a deafening chatter. Their movements were not unlike the uniform dartings of a school of minnows. The birds would wait for a favorable wind, say a front moving in from the northwest from Manitoba, and one day they would be gone save for a few addled stragglers.

Joseph rejected an impulse to circle the marsh and take a look at the coyote's den. The day was beginning to warm and it would be noon anyway before he made it back to the farm. He mounted awkwardly and realized he would have a sore ass, not having ridden this far in years. He idly hoped that the coyote would mate and the species would spread so that he might hear their howling on still nights. He had heard coyotes howl only once when he and the doctor had fished the Yellow Dog in the Upper Peninsula and he had thought it a wonderful sound, nearly as fine as the wail of the common loon, a cry so forlorn and pure it seemed from another planet.

Jim Harrison: Farmer

J oseph slumped deeply in the oversized bathtub which had been a gift from Arlice and the only noticeable luxury in the house. It had come only a few months before Carl died and he had steadfastly refused to use it preferring the metal tub that had always been placed in the middle of the kitchen floor on Saturday afternoons, with big kettles of water heating on the wood stove. Carl had said he would feel foolish in such a tub and his mother had amended that he was generally a bit silly on Saturday afternoons anyway, the sole even mildly critical statement Joseph had ever heard her address to him. He said you're right but continued bathing in the kitchen. Carl had caused a similar sort of problem in the thirties when the Rural Electrification Act brought power down their road and he had announced sententiously one evening at dinner that he wouldn't allow a hookup. It had taken a week of constant badgering by Joseph, his mother, and the doctor to get him to reconsider, and then he forbade any outlets in his bedroom, the barn, and the outbuildings. Carl thought of electricity as a fire hazard, ignoring the doctor's point that it was far less so than the kerosene lantern he used to milk with on dark winter mornings and evenings. The bedroom was a puzzle until he extended his edict to all the bedrooms: they were for sleeping not to dawdle around reading in. He was glad, however, to attend a succession of endless gatherings to celebrate the arrival of power.

Jim Harrison: Farmer

129

Joseph looked at the scar running down the inside of his leg from thigh to ankle. In places it zigzagged like lightning and at the knee the scar formed a knot, then continued rather thinly on down to his ankle where it made a left turn across the bridge of his foot. What a mess, he thought, but a mess appeared to be the rule of late. He smiled thinking of a banker in town, a friend of the doctor's. A few years back the banker's daughter had returned from college for summer vacation with a potter's wheel. She dug up clay and made three rather homely ordinary pots on the wheel, and growing tired of the difficulty, gave up the hobby. But one fateful Saturday when his golf game had been rained out, the banker tried his hand at the wheel and at present hadn't left it alone much except to sleep and eat. The banker took an early retirement which had been encouraged because his appearance had become shaggy and his behavior odd. He bought a kiln for his garage and when it hadn't met his standards he built a larger one outside. He spent a lot of time driving around in an old pickup digging up different sorts of clay. His wife and children abandoned him in disgust to his garage studio. Everyone felt sorry for them for having a lunatic husband and father. At first no one bought any of his pots and vases except the doctor who did so mostly to spite everyone. One day the banker stopped by the farm looking for clay. They had a drink and a chat and Joseph ordered a vase for Arlice. And Arlice who knew about such things had declared the vase first-rate. Joseph envied the man his obsessiveness about his pottery and glazes. The doctor had thought it sad that the man hadn't found what he loved to do until his mid-fifties though that was better than never finding it.

Joseph heard a car drive into the yard and his heartbeat quickened at the idea it might be Catherine. The image of her two appearances in his dreams made him giddy and he stood in the tub feeling hollow and vulnerable.

"Joseph?" It *was* her.

"I'm in the bathtub. Just a minute."

But she appeared at the door. "Daddy knows. When I

Jim Harrison: Farmer

———

started to leave just now he said I know where you're going, I heard you and Robert talking." She looked pale and distracted with all her whimsy gone. He was disappointed that she failed to resemble his dreams though it was difficult for him to admit it.

"I know. He came over here yesterday. We talked about it and at first I thought he was going to shoot me." Joseph laughed, toweling himself and trying to figure a way to change her mood.

"He said you weren't going to marry me and I was playing a fool." She burst into tears then and the tears quickly became deep sobs. "I still thought you might marry me but he said it would never happen. Joseph, I've given you the best single year of my life." She collapsed against the doorjamb.

"Oh bullshit." He yelled it but caught his profile in the mirror and that somehow slowed him down. "What the fuck were you going to do this year, fuck Robert? Look what I've done to my life." He grasped her shoulders and shook her to force her chin up. "You're playacting again for christ's sake."

She escaped him and threw herself sobbing onto the couch in the dining room. He hurriedly put on his pants wondering if she truly felt he would marry her or whether it was simply her best act yet.

"You know, Catherine," he began on a gentler tack, "we care a lot for each other and you have to think we've had some fine times together. But I'm a goddamn gimp forty-three-year-old schoolteacher farmer and you're lovely and bright and seventeen and want to be an actress. We can still be lovers when you go away. I mean when you come back." She sat up and smoothed back her hair; behind her tears the idea clearly appealed to her sense of drama.

"Well he seemed like he was trying to be mean, then he was nice saying I'd get over it, but I won't." Her chin still trembled and Joseph wondered how close her emotions were to the surface of her skin.

"He loves you. He just doesn't want you to marry an old

Jim Harrison: Farmer

man, which is sensible for any father." Joseph sat beside her and drew her to him as a father might but his intentions were owned by his dreams.

"I know I've caused him a lot of trouble," she snuffled. "I want us to be lovers like we were at first."

Now they lay back on the couch wordlessly agreeing that the nonsense was over, however real and unhappy. But the phone rang and Joseph jumped as if stung by a wasp.

"Hello!" He nearly shouted into the phone.

"Joseph, it's Arlice. What's wrong?"

"Nothing, nothing. Let me call you back in a half-hour, OK?" He was frantic to get off the phone and glanced at Catherine who was busy taking off her skirt. She mugged at him crazily.

"Fine. Be sure to call right back because I have to go out."

The receiver clicked and Joseph quickly took off his trousers. Catherine was sitting there with only her blouse on now and her penny loafers which she scuffed off. The gesture of the shoes and the white sleeveless blouse made her appear terribly naked. She lay back and unpinned her ponytail, drawing a foot up onto the couch. She wagged her knee back and forth and tapped the other foot. He stood there for a moment stunned at how lurid bodies could be in the clear afternoon light pouring through the windows. He turned to the dresser where Orin stared at them in his Air Force uniform, his hazel eyes too green in the tinted photo. The worn, flowered linoleum at his feet seemed to exude a fetor of kerosene mixed with sour milk, manure, rust, wet clothes, damp hay, though he had never noticed it before. Catherine held out a hand but her smile was frozen and thin with only the slightest suggestion of desire. Only her legs seemed to want him to come to the couch; her legs and sex were detached from her and he knelt down and put his face against them. She half crooned and half cried as Joseph was drawn surely back into his dream.

"Hello Arlice."

Jim Harrison: Farmer

"Christ, Joseph, I've been sitting here an hour. What were you doing? Is that girl there?"

"What girl?" He was shocked.

"Don't be cute, Joseph. Rosealee called me last night and I couldn't believe what she said only I have to. My god Yoey, why wait until now to fuck everything up?" Joseph felt poleaxed. He might have known that Rosealee would call Arlice. They had never lost touch. "Joseph are you there?"

"Yes." He tried to organize his thoughts but there were none. He glanced at Catherine who lay on the couch now completely nude. She had made them iced tea and was rubbing an ice cube on her belly and between her breasts, humming.

"Well if you can't say anything for yourself I will. I know you're taking the kids to Chicago tomorrow. I'm flying out and I'll be at the Drake by dinnertime. We're going to get this straightened out. That girl told Robert and Robert told Rosealee that you were going to marry the girl. Are you crazy?"

"No," he said, pausing too long, "I don't think so. I really can't talk now."

"Look Yoey, I know you have that despicable little cunt there right now so you can't talk. But you call the minute you get into town and then send all the kids except her somewhere. I want to see what you're ruining your life for. I'm sure from what Rosealee says that I understand her type."

"You ought to." Joseph was beginning to rebound in anger. Rosealee had once told Joseph how much Arlice liked the physical aspects of love though Joseph had already suspected as much.

"You dear bastard. I love you. Promise to call?"

"I guess so." He sighed as she offered a final I love you and hung up. My god. He couldn't refuse to see her because she was the dearest human in his life other than Rosealee. For twenty years she had somehow represented both the treachery and glory of what he thought of as the outside world. Once after a few drinks he had teased her about the age and condition of her

Jim Harrison: Farmer

———

husband and had been met with a smile and, that's OK, I've no problem finding lovers.

Outside of the novels he read, the word "lover" had always been mysterious to him. He felt that Rosealee and he were not really lovers but in the more mundane category labeled "going to get married." Save that single insane evening there had been no adventures in the profane. But now he had managed to become a living, breathing, sweating lover without really trying. It simply had happened upon him on an otherwise average October day and now in the first week of June it had become much less than a mixed blessing. She sprawled almost obscenely on the couch but he scarcely could chide her. It certainly wasn't obscene to Catherine. Despite her sense of the mortality of their affair, he was her lover and she meant to enjoy, rather, savor this refuge from boredom.

"This feels real strange," she giggled. She had placed an ice cube on her sex and raised up on her elbows rolling her eyes in some Chinese self-torture. "Try it."

"Jesus, no thanks." He stooped on the floor and pressed the ice cube firmly against her.

"Put it in then put yourself in." The idea swept her like a brainstorm.

"No thanks." He lifted the cube and began kissing her again but was repelled by the coolness. Death. Or it was against his nature? Then he kissed again, this time deeply rejecting his stodginess he hoped once and for all.

"I got a real talent for coming here at the wrong time." The doctor nosed the screen door then walked in.

"That's OK. Everyone on the goddamn earth knows my business. Even Arlice. She called. Rosealee told her. Now she's coming to Chicago."

"Well you might guess that, wouldn't you? I'll have a drink." The doctor sat down and glanced at Catherine who hadn't awakened. Joseph rose to cover her but suddenly felt it

Jim Harrison: Farmer

134

wasn't worth the effort. "You ever notice how many women surprise you when they're naked? Look at Catherine. She looks so slender in clothes but I must say she's beautiful without them. Of course I've seen thousands."

"You forget that I'm Yoey and a good boy." He laughed, giving his father's precise intonation for Yoey. "I haven't seen many."

"Well I'm not sure anyone is good in that sense. Some just act directly on their impulses while most of us ruminate like cows with four stomachs and a big ass. By the time you get through digesting the impulse, the impulse is gone. Don't you think? That's quite an idea. I'll drink to that idea. Jesus, old Major was pleased with that trout. All those wars and it takes a brown trout to thrill the piss out of him."

The doctor's face became cloudy and distracted. He glanced at Catherine again, then sighed and finished his drink. Joseph felt suddenly uncomfortable and naked in his trousers and stood to put his shirt on. A bluejay in the elm was screaming at a barn cat on the front porch, but the cat dozed on in a patch of shade behind a honeysuckle bush. The blossoming bush was full of bees and Joseph wondered if cats ever got stung.

"I guess I better deliver my lecture before she wakes up. I'm not sure I have a right to lecture you but I'm going to anyway. I have to step in here and tell you that you are being a number-one asshole. Don't you think so?" The doctor's voice was barely more than a whisper.

Joseph nodded, his temples burning. He envied the cat now making its way across the untrimmed lawn to the lilac thicket, unhurried, though the jay was dive-bombing toward him, shrieking and fluttering. The cat slid gracefully into the green world of the lilacs and the jay appeared satisfied.

"So I had to stop by Rosealee's and give her some pills so she could sleep. Oddly enough she thinks she has failed you, taking you for granted as being someone you have dem-

Jim Harrison: Farmer

135

onstrated you're not. Maybe that's a little true. It's our condition to be largely blind to one another unless jolted. You know why you like Catherine other than her obvious body there on the couch? It's because she is not even a person yet. You've given her nothing and even if you had there would be nothing there in return. And it's because she hasn't anything to return yet except her body. Think of living with the major and that alcoholic wife. Who wouldn't turn to you?" The doctor got up and made himself another drink, placing the bottle on the table. "And you show all the signs of cracking up. You didn't bird hunt with any interest last fall and you've hardly fished this spring. And it wasn't your mother. The life is draining out of you. You're a strong person and when a strong person fucks up they do so with a vengeance."

"Look, you can ease off. I know you're right and I thought when I brought the kids back I would close up here and drive off somewhere and think it over." The idea of driving off was an appealing lie. Joseph immediately pictured himself in some far-off place in a tent by the ocean where everything would be clear and definite as bad weather.

"That's precisely what you can't do. What does thinking things over mean? It is a process by which you will attempt to get yourself out of the gun seat, off the hook. And it's too late to do that. Far too late. I don't mean your age but the other person."

"I know what you want is I should simply marry Rosealee. I can be the ghost of Orin and give her a wonderful life." Joseph laughed and drank straight from the bottle but the doctor was angry.

"Oh fuck the ghost of Orin. That's what's wrong with you in part. Orin is dead. Dead meat, deader than the major's fish, dead like you and I will be someday not all that distant from us. Rosealee is alive. She's three miles up the road and she is probably wondering why she gave her life over to a goddamn lunatic."

Jim Harrison: Farmer

—————

Now Joseph thought his head would burst and he began walking in circles around the room averting his eyes from Catherine who had begun to snore softly. "You see I know you're right but I can know what's right and feel paralyzed. I knew last autumn when I was looking for that coyote and sitting there so many hours. I'd been in that same place twenty years before once with Dad rabbit hunting. And I said what have I done those twenty years? I had the feeling I was hiding out and you can't talk yourself out of hiding somewhere. It just came like a flash. Like the coyote took the chicken in a blur but the notion didn't stay long enough to convince me. Like you say I was a cow putting it through my four stomachs."

"What are you guys talking about?" Catherine was awake. She slipped on her skirt and walked sleepily to the bathroom. She frowned in irritation as if being awakened too early for school.

"What I mostly meant is that I'm not saying you should marry Rosealee. No. I didn't say that." The doctor was excited and thunked the bottle against the table to emphasize his words. "No I didn't say that. Only you shouldn't drag out whatever your sense of punishment might be. You might think she's punished you which is false. She is only being alive with an honesty you're not capable of. You are thinking like you're turning a golf ball over and over trying to decide which side is which. My god, Joseph, you have to act some other way than sitting here thinking that life has jilted you. That's what I mean. If you want to marry, marry, and if not say Rosealee I can't marry you. Just do something other than walking around this place pissing your life away brooding."

Catherine came from the bathroom and looked out the screen door. "It's going to rain." She turned to them still without bra or blouse. "Don't pay any attention to me. I know you're having an important talk." Her nipples were small and reddish brown, almost childlike on her modest breasts. She took a Coke from the refrigerator, slipped on her blouse, and

Jim Harrison: Farmer

———

137

went out on the porch swing and began humming. They both paused to stare at her through the window, perhaps wanting to disbelieve her presence but the porch swing creaked and her humming merged with and amplified the bees.

"Of course I'm not really all that goddamn smart myself. Old people mostly aren't wise, they're just old. It's like they can say, do a lot, do a lot because you're going to get old and die. They no longer live in the future because there's not much of it left. You said you remembered rabbit hunting in that place with your dad, the place where you looked for the coyote and then twenty years had passed. Right. But I walked around the marsh to that place more than twenty years further back than you and I feel the same way. What happened I wonder. But everyone thinks these thoughts though they don't talk about it much. It's funny but I mostly keep track of the past by remembering what bird dog I owned in what period. And now it's too late to own one at all. I can't ask a high-spirited pointer to sit on its ass and watch me disintegrate." The doctor laughed at the idea and his laughter released Joseph from his impossible tension.

"Rosealee said she wanted to talk when I get back from Chicago. That's in three days, you know. If I don't make up my mind by then you can chloroform me and chop off my good leg. Is that a fair bargain?"

"No. Who wants your goddamn leg?"

They were cast into silence by Catherine's singing a popular song in a thin but rather good voice. It was a slow mournful song about unhappy love. Joseph would have preferred a jay screaming at the cat again; he remembered painfully the way Arlice and Rosealee were always singing together. They knew dozens of songs and on summer evenings they were sometimes allowed to walk over to the pavilion on a lake that doubled as a dance hall and roller-skating rink. Orin and he would tag along throwing stones at fence posts and birds while the girls sang. They pretended out of embarrassment that they disliked the

Jim Harrison: Farmer

138

singing but Joseph secretly thought it wonderful. They would sit down on the dock while the girls skated to the pipe organ music. There was a concession that rented rowboats and they talked to the fishermen coming in in the gathering dark. The organist would vary slow waltzes with zippy jazz tunes and marches and it was absurd the way the music changed the mood as they sat on the dock. Joseph always suspected that Orin wouldn't skate because Joseph wasn't able to but Orin insisted he hated the thought of it. And walking home in the dark the singing was even better with the smell of drying hay, the weed-choked ditches, and frogs croaking. Where the road passed through the swamp they often flushed partridge and it always alarmed them. Why couldn't Orin have chosen Arlice leaving Rosealee for me? It would have been natural.

The doctor was standing up staring at him. "Where have you been? Back on the couch with her or with someone else?" He was smiling though.

"I was thinking about the way the girls used to sing all the time." But he lost touch again for a moment. Arlice didn't like Orin or he might have been willing. So maybe it's her fault but I don't think she wanted me to have nothing. She simply didn't like Orin that way.

The doctor said good-bye, then on his way out the drive beeped and waved at Catherine on the porch. She waved back and came into the house still humming.

"I just imagined I was your daughter and the doctor came to tell you I was pregnant." She giggled. "Only it was too hard to see you as my dad." She took off her blouse and put it on the table with the Coke bottle.

"Oh jesus what you dream of. You'll end up in the loony bin."

"You're sort of crazy yourself from what I heard." She sat on his lap and there was a trace of the scent of honeysuckle on her shoulder. "But he's a good doctor and he's helping Mother some. During the Korean War she would just sit around in our

Jim Harrison: Farmer

---

apartment brooding like you do and the only way she could get happy was to sit around drinking scotch with the other wives. We didn't see Dad for almost two years and when he got home she was an A-1 drunk. Period. So were some of the other women. That's why I'm never going to drink whiskey. Period."

She twisted on the chair, straddling his lap and kissing him.

"I don't think I want to again." It was a lie though.

"Of course if you marry Rosealee we can't be lovers. But I'll probably understand." She unfastened her skirt and hiked it farther up her waist. "Let's do it this way."

"I bet you wouldn't marry me if I asked. You're just using me until you can get out of town." Joseph was teasing but her face darkened and tears came to her eyes.

Jim Harrison: Farmer

———

After Catherine left to go home for dinner Joseph had an unpleasant phone call from Karen's father saying she couldn't be allowed to go on the senior trip because he had "heard certain things." Joseph spent a solid half-hour talking the man out of his decision. Bruce, Karen's father, had been an energetic reprobate until his mid-thirties when he was saved at a revival and became a Nazarene. They had known each other since childhood and Joseph forced himself to be relaxed and devious, even using the Bible to talk about the gossips who "bore false witness" against others out of guilt over their own sin. Joseph couldn't stand the idea that Karen would miss the trip because of him. She had spent the last month or so reading about Chicago and had decided to spend her day and a half in the Field Museum of Natural History and the Aquarium. Joseph had looked forward to joining her.

Through the years he had made a half-dozen trips to Chicago with the seniors and had always been disappointed when they chose Detroit. He loved the museum and was usually boggled for days afterward and the ball game provided a nice relief to the museum, though Robert and Catherine intended to skip the ball game and see a play. So Joseph overwhelmed Bruce by wit, agreeing that Bruce could come over after they returned and "talk about the Lord Jesus and what He could do for you." Karen was home free; he was mindful that it might provide the big event of her life, her sole trip out of northern Michigan into the outside world.

After the phone call he drove over to the lake and filled up with gas to be ready for their early morning departure. There were cars parked outside the pavilion and he could hear the skating music from the gas station, only now it was on record. That was the only difference. He was surprised to see Catherine and Robert walk jauntily in with their skates over their shoulders. He ducked behind the gas pump but they were unaware of everything except what they were talking about. The lake was rough in a warm but strong south wind, rare for June when the evenings were usually the stillest of the year.

He drove the back roads for the hour just before dark and when he passed the log trail going off through the pine barrens from the gravel road he considered having another try at the coyote. But he was exhausted and had left his brace at home, and knew anyway that the coyote would be jittery in such a strong wind. He passed a dozen deserted farms with tangled orchards, the broken windows of the houses forming black holes, and some with the barns leaning and creaking in the wind. It was a naked land, nearly gutted with sand blowing through ferns and brake. It never should have been farmed at all; it was so marginal that the only truly green grass grew up beside the barns in places once owned by manure piles. It was a sad trick played on those who had moved north a half-century before and who hadn't known good land from bad, or were too poor to buy the good. Joseph remembered some of them; the few who were left in the twenties were driven out finally in the thirties. Occasionally the farm houses would be tenanted for a year or so by the bitterly poor, the half-mad retarded sort who hung on the fringe of any farm community existing on the oddest of temporary jobs and the county dole and the guilty concern of neighbors who had somehow held on.

In his youth these people had been held up by his father as the true unfortunates. Once one of their children, a little girl,

Jim Harrison: Farmer

had fallen from a rickety flatbed truck in front of their farm and the people had been embarrassed and said, she's fine, when the child was white from pain and her arm badly scraped. The man was thin and his eyes were watery and the wife never looked up from her feet while she held the child waiting for the doctor on the front porch. The other children played on the tire swing and his mother served them all some food and lemonade. Carl gave the man a drink and the man said they had had a string of bad luck. He stared at the radio and Joseph remembered that his wife smiled shyly when Carl turned it on. They had some ham and the man said it was fine ham so they went out to look at the smokehouse. Then they went down into the cellar and Carl gave the man a smoked ham that weighed maybe thirty pounds and said everyone gets down on their luck, once in Chicago when I came to this country I ate bread for two weeks looking for work. Joseph saw them only once more and that was in September when their whole family was picking potatoes for a neighbor, even the small girl with a broken arm in the cold rainy field with her sisters scrambling around putting the potatoes into crates.

Then the family disappeared and no one knew what happened to them. On that last day when Carl stopped, when they were picking potatoes, Joseph gave one of the daughters who was his age, about ten, his polished Petoskey stone an aunt had given him for Christmas the year before. She had accepted it with a hand muddy from her potato picking. Beneath the mud the hand looked cold and chapped and red.

Now the wind was blowing even harder and the setting sun cast a yellowish pall over the landscape. There was a horse far out in a pasture, butt to the wind with its tail blowing through its legs along its belly. Horses somehow always hated a strong wind and either lay down or turned their back quarters to it. What had happened to the girl and did she still have the stone? Like Catherine and Robert entering the skating rink—he wondered at the lives people led outside the field of his perceptions.

Jim Harrison: Farmer

He turned toward home and passed a pale green field surrounded by a stump fence. He had demolished such a fence with Carl, pulling the huge white pine stumps with the team of horses toward a central place and burning them on a rainy day so the fire wouldn't spread. The only unpleasant aspect was that there were so many snakes living in the fence; garter snakes, blue racers, and milk snakes. Some lived in the stumps themselves and when the fire was started with kerosene they came sliding out in unbelievable numbers and the horses shied. Joseph and Carl had quickly moved out of the field and into the road to watch the fire. He had never minded snakes but when so many were around it was nightmarish.

About a mile from home Joseph stopped in front of the last deserted farm before the land became acceptably fertile again. There was a long row of Lombardy poplars along the front of the property and the wind whipped the undersides of their leaves to a silver froth. The sun was huge and red and sinking into the state forest. Joseph smiled remembering that when he was very young he believed the sun sank in the field out behind the barn.

When he walked into the house the phone was ringing and he swore at the idea that it might be Bruce changing his mind. But it was Rosealee.

"Hello Joseph. I wanted to wish you a fine time in Chicago. I'll have Robert ready on time." Her voice began to waver and she breathed deeply. "I love you, Joseph."

"I love you, Rosealee." He cleared his throat but found nothing more to say.

"Will I see you on Wednesday night?" Then she lost her voice again. "I guess I can't talk now." It was a barely audible whisper.

"Wednesday night," he said. "Can I come now?"

"No. Please not now. I'm a mess. I love you. Good-bye."

When he went to bed a sigh escaped him that was close to a

shudder then became a shudder and he had difficulty breathing. In the light cast by the bedlamp the room was unnaturally clear and defined, as were his arms and chest when he looked down at them. *Oh god what is happening now?* He couldn't be sick because he had to start for Chicago with the kids at dawn. But his stomach felt fine and after the hard breathing his body felt strangely at peace. He got up and turned on the lights and walked around the house. It seemed he was looking at much of the house for the first time, or was in the process of recognizing it from a dream. In the bathroom he looked in the mirror and there was the sense of shock his father always described when he hit a hidden stone point-blank with the plow blade. *Jesus that's me.* He shaved then to avoid having to do it in the morning, whistling loudly, and sang a hymn because he couldn't remember any other songs. But he sang the hymn as if it were the most maudlin of love songs, stretching the words in inappropriate places. Whatever was happening to him now wasn't at all unpleasant. He decided to test this new mood and rushed to his mother's bedroom. There were a number of photos of Carl on the wall above the dresser that he habitually avoided looking at when he entered the room. One of them showed Carl holding a large pike by the gills and grinning with Joseph beside him in bare feet holding a stringer of bluegills. It was only a photo of "them," objective. But the wedding picture brought a smile because Carl looked so stiff and terrified next to his mother's calm beauty.

Back in the dining room he rejected an impulse to have a nightcap. He wanted to see if the mood would maintain itself. In bed he turned off the light and anticipated that he would return to normal in the dark. But maybe he *had* returned to normal. He searched out the day that Carl lay wet and dead on the river bank with the car overturned down by the pilings of the bridge. A man stood there. He was wet and he said, I pulled him out but he was dead as a mackerel. The doctor was crying and said heart attack over and over. He hugged Joseph and the funeral-home man came and took Carl away. Joseph forced

Jim Harrison: Farmer

himself through the terrors of the following three days as if he were looking at a movie, but though he breathed more deeply he could still handle it without pushing the images away. His mother's funeral had been so calm and peaceful in contrast, everyone she knew sitting in church with the knowledge of her death already in their heads for six months. Nearly everyone in the church was very old except her children and grandchildren and Rosealee. Even her oldest daughter had gray hair. There were no surprises here, and after they all had dinner at the Grange Hall, which was the custom, Joseph greeted each person and noted their quiet affability. At his father's funeral there had been wailing.

On the edge of sleep he saw Rosealee whispering to him on the phone and the choking sensation returned to his throat. The ache dissipated as he entered the heady country that exists on the verge of the first dream but the dream was a memory. *Arlice and Rosealee and the fruitpickers near the cattle barns at the fair. The fruitpickers were Mexicans and they had a band made up of guitars, an accordion, and a trumpet. They played in the afternoon for the collection when they passed the hat. The girls loved the music, were drawn up into it, and losing their caution they began to dance. The fruitpickers smiled and the farmers and children gathered in a circle and clapped for them. The dust rose around their legs and though it was hot they danced on and on until Carl came and made them stop.* He drifted back into wakefulness, from the dust that encircled them like smoke, as he remembered his jealousy when he thought the men were looking at the girls wrongly. What a time he had trying to sleep after they went swimming in the pond by the marsh with Rosealee drawing on her underpants and then her dress which became damp. It was a mystery because they were invisible. So were sharks because nobody had quite figured them out, like the planets. The kids were never interested in the planets because in any real sense they simply did not believe the planets existed though on tests they went

Jim Harrison: Farmer

through the motions. Robert reading science fiction all the time believed in planets, even that creatures lived on planets in other galaxies. And flying saucers that were spying on us, perhaps making contact with some people who kept it a secret out of fear. Maybe he was right about that at least. One summer evening after the war he and Orin and Rosealee drank a lot and took little Robert to the free show that was held next to the tavern, a noisy projector casting the movie on a large sheet. Robert and Orin went to sleep on the blanket but the movie was *Mutiny on the Bounty* with Charles Laughton, and Joseph looked at the sea with eagerness. His hand touched Rosealee's and they clasped but he paid no attention. She lay drowsily against his chest her thigh against his and he was abruptly torn from the movie. I'm cold she had said moving closer with lavender rising from her hair. Then her hand touched his lap and recoiled, lay lightly against his chest, and she gave him a light kiss and laughed. He had walked into the tavern then out of shame until he could calm down.

Jim Harrison: Farmer

*T*he children spread out across the pasture picking milkweed pods. There were only thirty of them in grades one through twelve, the entire school. Joseph sat in the middle of the field directing operations, perched on a rock pile. The youngest children were unhappy because those in the upper grades beat them to the pods. They wept piteously. It was a hot day in September and Joseph's handkerchief was damp with his own sweat and the tears of the little ones. A group of high school girls approached and announced that Marcia had to pee. Marcia was a trifle slow and giggled all the time. She was fat and never wore socks with her usually filthy flour-sack dresses. Her people were poor. Joseph waved them off toward a basswood swale. The older boys were in the far corner of the pasture dragging full gunny sacks. They had been scuffling all day to see who filled the most sacks. The milkweed pods were needed for life preservers for the war effort. Or so he was told. The war was in its fourth year and Joseph was sure it would never stop.

Jim Harrison: Farmer

———

His sense of clear-headed strength persisted into the early morning hours. He knew he needed it for the massive assault on his senses that was coming in the next two days. At least there were only five seniors this year. Once on a trip to Detroit there had been twelve and three of the boys had got so drunk that Joseph had called Dr. Evans long distance the next morning fearing alcohol poisoning, when two of them continued with the dry heaves. The doctor prescribed a large creme de menthe on the rocks and it had worked too well; the second night the same boys threw cherry bombs from the hotel window and launched a small rocket that had hit the window sill and reversed into the room, doing moderate damage. Luckily one of the arresting officers was also from northern Michigan and was understanding about the peculiarities of a "senior trip" as a sort of rite of passage during which even ordinarily calm students had a tendency to go nuts.

He picked up Karen first, at dawn, and was appalled to see Bruce standing with her in the driveway, a goose protecting a gosling that no one wanted. Joseph put her small cardboard suitcase in the trunk and was irritated to find Bruce staring at him sternly. He would have it out with this asshole when the occasion arose. Bruce made sure that Karen had taken her Bible and they were off. Karen was in her best clothes which emphasized her large ungainly figure. She sat in the back,

Jim Harrison: Farmer

———

149

probably assuming that he would prefer to sit next to someone else.

Everyone was ready and waiting except Catherine. Lisa loaded with perfume and her face swollen with sleep; Daniel in a cheap new suit beaming like an idiot with his parents standing beside him and tears in his mother's eyes (he had never been away from home before); Robert standing alone in his red jacket, new saddle shoes, and charcoal gray trousers holding a paperback book and Orin's leather suitcase. They had to wait ten minutes for Catherine, and everyone fidgeted as the major came out to apologize and began talking about fishing with Joseph. When Catherine came running out and claimed the seat next to Joseph the major said, well, keep track of her, with just a trace of irony.

"Oh god you're wearing suspenders," Catherine said and they all laughed.

Joseph sadly lost most of his newfound sense of ease within the first hundred miles. Catherine was by turns possessive, bitchy, conspiratorial, and Joseph noted by the reaction of the others that their secret was now fully in the open. Catherine fiddled with the radio until he had to firmly shut it off, then she let her hand rest on his thigh which caused Robert, sitting on the other side of her, to stare out the window in embarrassment. The blood surged to Joseph's face and he sensed deeply what a complete fool he had been to have an affair with a student. But then she twisted to talk to those in the back seat with her skirt hiking up her thighs and he felt a helpless pull of lust again, mixed with despair over so foully complicating his life. He would have gladly shoved her from the speeding car.

His spirits lifted somewhat after he began an aggressive dialogue with Karen about birds and was amazed again at her knowledge. She told how she had gone up to Grayling with her father to look at cattle and had been lucky enough to see a Kirtland's warbler, a bird whose sole habitat, other than its winter migration, was a county in northern Michigan. Ornithologists

Jim Harrison: Farmer

150

estimated that there were less than a thousand of them. When they stopped for gas Catherine had insisted on getting in the back seat out of disgust for the turn in conversation. Robert joined her and Karen and Daniel moved to the front seat. Lisa was sleeping and snoring loudly. Robert complained but Joseph said to leave her alone.

He took great pains to keep Karen talking, to draw her out further, but when she did talk she was shy and kept her eyes cast down. She had seen a marsh hawk take a rabbit but the rabbit had been too heavy for the hawk to carry away so the hawk had fed on it boldly just a hundred yards or so behind their barn. When she lapsed into silence Joseph began a long monologue on the sea; a book he especially prized was Darwin's *Voyage of the Beagle*, and the mysteries of the Pacific between Peru and Ecuador, and the distant Galapagos which fascinated him. The confluence of the Humboldt and El Niño currents was off Ecuador and that caused a prodigious upswelling of marine life. A man had caught a black marlin weighing nearly fifteen hundred pounds. Then he talked about the sea off Tierra del Fuego which had been called the "Serengeti of the marine world." This had puzzled him until he remembered that the writer Ernest Hemingway had talked about the Serengeti with its vast game populations in *Green Hills of Africa*. He had liked that book and when he had insisted in a letter that Arlice read it she replied she wasn't interested in hunting stories. Joseph had been angry and had thought that at least in hunting you see things, you are not simply walking around scratching your ass. He paused in his talking to remember the name of the Hemingway novel about the love affair with the nurse named Catherine who was so unlike the Catherine he had dallied with. The book had upset him terribly and the night he had finished it he had had trouble sleeping. Karen said she had been angry when her brother, who was a notorious violator, and a friend had shot seventy ducks one day the fall before and had told her not to tell the teacher.

By midafternoon they were checked into their hotel, a

Jim Harrison: Farmer

151

modest but clean place off the Loop. Daniel seemed the most dazed, and strangely hung onto Karen for authority. She had never received any attention from a man and turned a bit flirtatious which surprised Joseph. The Field Museum would still be open for three hours but Catherine and Robert tried to beg off. Lisa said she wanted to go to some stores. Joseph bought them maps feeling well rid of them. He told them to be back at six for dinner which was part of the package the hotel offered. The hotels were wise enough to offer their grubbiest for these senior excursions except to the teachers or chaperones whose return business they sought.

They had a fine time at the Field Museum with Daniel full of admiration for Karen saying you know a helluva a lot. He had taken to holding her hand. Joseph remembered that he had to call Arlice and went off to a pay phone. He dreaded his confrontation with her and was frantic getting change when several people seemed to stare at him. Arlice wanted him to bring Catherine and Robert over for dinner but Joseph said they had to eat together at the hotel because they had already paid for it and besides he suspected they all wanted to go to a movie. Arlice merely said nonsense bring them by seven. At least she couldn't get murderous with him if Catherine and Robert were there. He rejoined Karen and Daniel who were looking at a huge dinosaur skeleton. Daniel was wondering aloud if their meat had been good to eat because there sure was a lot of it. Daniel packed the largest lunch in the whole school and willingly cleaned up the unwanted sandwiches of the others.

Back at the hotel he was startled to see Robert talking with familiarity to a stranger, a finely dressed man in his midtwenties. Catherine was cool but nervous with him when he said they had to visit Arlice but her interest picked up when he added that Arlice was having two old friends from her theater days over for her and Robert to meet. When he washed up for dinner some of the clarity of the evening before returned to him. He was disturbed by the luxury of his room but it occur-

Jim Harrison: Farmer

152

red to him that this was the last trip of this sort that he would ever take. He sat on the soft bed with his hands clasped wondering what Rosealee was doing. She liked teaching far better than he, worked with heart and energy. But he hadn't been all that bad for twenty years; sometimes he rambled on with such enthusiasm that the spread of it had to take someone in. The professor that summer at Ann Arbor had said that the only good teachers were those who taught with passion. Passion was commonly understood among even the stupidest of people. If you couldn't be passionate about the knowledge you were giving to younger, susceptible people, you should get out of the way for people who could be. Joseph had been impressed though it was obvious to him that the idea was more viable on a college level. Some of his farm kids were so exhausted from the work they did before and after school they could scarcely stay awake for their lesson. This had led Joseph throughout his life to regard knowledge, especially knowledge that couldn't be directly applied, as a secret vice, a source of beauty and enthusiasm that, however, didn't get the chores done or make the mortgage payment. But over the years a few students such as Karen had brought him a solid sort of pleasure and the sudden thought that Samuel was somewhere in Chicago brought him joy.

He sorted through an envelope to make sure he had enough tickets for the ball game the following night. George Kell, Hoot Evers, Vic Wertz, Johnny Lipon. In the late thirties he and Einar and Carl had seen Hank Greenberg hit a bases-loaded home run. Einar had private theories about Jews and Hank Greenberg disturbed him. The Baptist minister had recently assured everyone that the Palestinian war and the return of the Jews to their ancient homeland meant the end of the world and the Second Coming of Christ was near at hand. Einar quite simply didn't want the world to end just when he was building up a first-rate dairy herd.

We are such stupid bastards Joseph thought. The kids star-

Jim Harrison: Farmer

———

153

ing wide-eyed at the blacks in Chicago because there were none back home other than an occasional transient laborer in the summer. He wondered if they were all stupid because they never went anywhere, but people in Chicago were probably stupid in another way. How could he be messed up when everyone was apparently messed up? Messed up was the norm and the peace and mindful ease he sought were rare and only the doctor came close. Maybe it was because he was so busy healing and when he wasn't healing he was fishing, hunting, drinking, eating, reading, or playing pinochle. And thinking; but the doctor's thinking doesn't anchor him like a rowboat as mine does. He sails away from thought to thought scarcely pausing. Samuel might turn out like the doctor. The doctor thought the source of most unhappiness was that nearly everyone wanted to be someplace or someone else. At the end of his working day at the office and hospital the doctor always had a glass of fine bourbon which he sipped with such enthusiasm that it pleased Joseph to watch; then if there were enough energy left he would cook some strange sort of food, often with enough garlic to fill the nose.

Joseph and Catherine and Robert walked the ten or so blocks to the Drake with Catherine petulant, slowing for shop windows that caught her fancy, and Robert distracted and restive. They saw a black man in a chauffeur's uniform walking a Borzoi and were thrilled because they had never seen such a strange-looking dog. Catherine asked the man what sort of dog it was and he said Borzoi as if only an utter fool wouldn't know. The man wore sunglasses though the sun had descended behind the buildings. They waited for a red light and Robert mentioned that he hoped he wouldn't have to stay too long because he had some things he wanted to do.

"Look Robert, I thought you liked Arlice. If you don't want to see her I don't give a shit what you do. You can go down to the lake and drown yourself." Joseph felt strained and

Jim Harrison: Farmer

thought how fine it would be to whap Robert over the head with his cane.

"Oh god don't get so mad." Robert looked down the street past the Drake to the park and Lake Michigan as if he were considering jumping in the lake. It was a warm, still evening and they could see a number of sailboats with slack sails, barely moving.

"You're not going to meet Richard until nine," Catherine said in what she assumed was a sophisticated stage voice.

"It's not that I don't want to be with you people. You're fine but I've been with you so long and I want to see some-one else."

Joseph shrugged and kept walking, then he turned and waved to Robert who stood there with Catherine, and looked so desolate that it drew on Joseph's sympathy. "I understand, Robert. Have a fine time and don't get lost. What you do is your business." Catherine ran to catch up and took Joseph's arm. They paused for a few moments and watched Robert walk stiffly back down the street.

The lobby of the Drake was so elegant to Joseph that it gave him tunnel vision. Impatient waiting for the elevator, it occurred to him he didn't know the number of Arlice's room. Then he was strident when he got the room number from the clerk, who was civil, being accustomed to eccentrics. Catherine made a convincing attempt at being blasé and grab-bed Joseph's hand as he beat his cane noisily against the floor waiting for the elevator.

He was appalled when Arlice opened the door and she was red-eyed and sniffling and two men stood behind her smiling. But she was gracious to Catherine, explaining that they had been talking about her first husband who had lost his life in Spain. She said when she introduced the men that they had been in the Shakespeare repertory company with her husband and they had spent the afternoon talking about old times and perhaps drinking a little too much. Joseph hastily poured a

Jim Harrison: Farmer

glass of whiskey and moved to the window which afforded a grand view of the park and Lake Michigan. It was easy to imagine that it was the sea. He drained the whiskey quickly to calm himself. Jesus, he thought someone had died and Arlice was usually so gay. One of the men gave Catherine some champagne and she sat with them talking animatedly. He felt a little ashamed when he suspected with relief that Arlice might be too upset to make it unpleasant for him.

"Joseph." Arlice beckoned to him from a door. He hadn't noticed that they were in a drawing room without beds. He followed her into the bedroom, first topping off his glass. "Well darling what have you got to say?" She came into his arms and he lifted her as he always did.

"Nothing. I'm not going to say anything. You should know I'm not going to answer to you any more than you'd answer to me." He went to the window for another view of the lake; it was nearly fishless, the sea lamprey having wiped out the lake trout. "But if you want to just talk, fine. I'll talk."

"She's rather pretty. Much prettier than I thought she would be. I somehow imagined you belting some fat farm girl in the hay even though Rosealee said that she was pretty." Arlice sat on the bed holding her face in her hands. Then she flopped back with her hands behind her head. "I called Rosealee and she said you had told the doctor you would make up your mind before you came back. Is that true?" She rose to her elbows and her stare was cold, demanding an answer.

"Yes. Of course." Joseph was amazed again at what went on beyond his vision. He hadn't suspected that the doctor and Rosealee were talking about such things. But why not? "I've proven myself best at dragging things out."

"What do you think you'll decide?" Now she came to the window and stood beside him. They used to stand by the window watching the snow fall and guessing how deep the drifts would become. When he spent those months in bed with his injury she would come home from school and pretend to be a

Jim Harrison: Farmer

156

nurse, waiting upon him, bringing him cookies, chatting about school, and going over the assignments so he wouldn't fall behind.

"There's nothing to decide. I always intended to marry her. In a way there's no choice. There's not much choice in what I'm going to do anyway because I have to make a living. Maybe I'll fall asleep and the goddamn tractor will tip over on top of me." Nothing he said surprised him though he hadn't voiced it before. "I'm not exactly old yet."

"Who said you were?" she laughed. "But you do have a choice. Rosealee wouldn't want you to marry her because you had no choice."

"Oh bullshit. That's not what I mean. I meant what else do I know how to do? I taught and that's over and I know how to farm and that's fine. I just won't be a real farmer is all. I'll put in one crop of wheat or corn at Orin's and ours and then I'll do what I want in the time left. Rosealee wants to teach in town."

Arlice hugged him again in relief. "Why didn't you tell her that? Was it that girl who made you wait?" She looked in a dresser mirror and began to repair her face. "If you knew that was what you were going to do it was cruel for you to make her wait so long."

"I wasn't sure." He was becoming angry again. "Why the fuck should I be so taken for granted? You do what you want and you all had these grand ideas about what I should do from the beginning. I'm not you and you aren't me. Neither of us is Rosealee." He was beating the cane against the radiator to emphasize his words. "Anyway I'll have to be an improvement over Orin but if I want to take off for a while in the winter I'm going to."

"That girl out there doesn't make you much of an improvement over Orin." She laughed, recognizing that the side she had come to Chicago to defend had so effortlessly proved the winner. Joseph knew this but cared less. The warm still evening outside the window made him want to be at home or

Jim Harrison: Farmer

157

trout fishing or sitting on the porch swing with Rosealee with their laps perhaps covered with the glossy equipment catalogs that had been such an integral part of their lives. Any talk about the future was always full of catalogs and maps. Should it be a Massey-Ferguson, John Deere, or Farmall and was it to be Oregon or Florida or Georgia on their first trip to a coast.

"I sure enough haven't piled up Orin's numbers. One isn't too many I don't think. I wanted to be carried away, you know? I didn't think of that when we started last fall but that was what kept me going. One night Rosealee and I got carried away for the first time since we were young. I mean we were doing something we didn't actually know we were going to do before we did it."

Arlice was amused and had become relaxed again. She thanked him for shipping the trunks which she had always wanted. They lapsed into gossip and Joseph lay down on the bed in a hopeless attempt to rid himself of the effects of the whiskey. Arlice took off her dress and put on a robe and Joseph mentioned that she hadn't totally lost her figure yet. They went back into the living room and one of Arlice's friends raised his eyebrows in mock concern. The men were so elegant that Joseph momentarily wished he had left his suspenders back in the room as Catherine had advised. She had drunk far too much champagne and her natural coquettishness had gotten out of hand though the men didn't pay any attention.

By the time they left he had to support Catherine and he could barely support himself. One of the actors had been a marvelous storyteller and after enough drinks had been able to draw Joseph into telling some extravagantly obscene stories of country life, many of them originating with the doctor who knew everyone's business. Arlice had fallen asleep in her chair but woke as they said good-bye. She kissed him and asked why didn't he call Rosealee. He told her not to get pushy.

In the cab Catherine's head lolled and she became hysterical when Joseph thought they had better not sleep together as

Jim Harrison: Farmer

planned. They were both too drunk and tomorrow night would be better.

"Oh please you promised. Goddamn you. You promised," she yelled. The cabby kept glancing in the mirror and muttering, probably wondering whether or not she was going to vomit in his cab.

When they got to the room there was a note from Daniel under the door saying that Robert wasn't back yet and he was worried. It was three a.m. and Joseph thought, let him worry, though Daniel probably just wanted to talk to someone. Catherine stripped and stumbled to the bathroom. He took a pint from his suitcase and poured a large drink. He felt no desire for Catherine and he meant to stun himself into sleep. He lay back sipping his drink and reading a catalog from the Field Museum though the words blurred and he couldn't connect the sense of the sentences and the slippery brochure was hard to hold. He felt distant from the sounds of Catherine being sick. It had been a fine evening for her after perhaps a dull year in which he had been the only diversion. He acknowledged his position as a diversion though he knew she never would. Now he felt pity for her, even liked her for the pain she felt. He went into the bathroom and found her half moaning, half dozing against the toilet bowl. He lifted her into the shower and she mumbled that she loved him. He turned on the water and supported them both under the stream but it didn't help. She giggled as he toweled her and fell promptly asleep when he carried her to bed. He had expected a whirling sleepless night but he too became nothing when his head touched the pillow.

Dawn. A soiled, yellowish light comes in the window. It is cloudy. A nude girl stands next to the bed. She rubs her face hard and sighs. She goes into the bathroom and looks into a shaving kit for aspirin and takes three. She nearly retches with the water but it passes. The water tastes like chlorine, vomit, and wine. She shakes the man awake.

Jim Harrison: Farmer

"Joseph I feel terrible."

"Of course." He squints and rolls on his back. It is too warm in the room. Why is he in bed with Catherine? He begins to lapse back into sleep but she notices he is erect and covers him with some effort. It is pleasant to him but his dreams are with another. He should call her right now. It will wait, and he looks up at the girl sitting on him with love. She seems on the verge of sleep and slumps forward and begins crying. He comforts her until they are unjoined and she sleeps again. He thinks for a moment about the actor and how once when he was reading to his class he was so carried away everyone was enthused. Carried away where? He begins to sleep but thinks of the horse that died and Rosealee sitting up on it with his mother standing by the pump shed telling her to be careful. Arlice is standing there too and Carl is sitting on the steps rolling a cigarette. Joseph stands against the grape arbor watching Rosealee in her flower-print dress and bare feet trot the horse around the barnyard. *She slows the horse by the grape arbor and he takes the halter and she smiles at him, the miniature violets on her cotton dress*

Jim Harrison: Farmer